W9-CFG-746

Gravity

Gravity

Leanne
Lieberman

ORCA BOOK PUBLISHERS

Library and Archives Canada Cataloguing in Publication

Lieberman, Leanne, 1974-
Gravity / written by Leanne Lieberman.

ISBN 978-1-55469-049-7

I. Title.
PS8623.I36G73 2008   jC813'.6   C2008-903058-3

First published in the United States, 2008

Library of Congress Control Number: 2008928573

Summary: An Orthodox Jewish teenager comes to terms with her sexuality and her faith.

Orca Book Publishers gratefully acknowledges the support for its publishing programs
provided by the following agencies: the Government of Canada through the Book
Publishing Industry Development Program and the Canada Council for the Arts,
and the Province of British Columbia through the BC Arts Council
and the Book Publishing Tax Credit.

Cover and text design by Teresa Bubela
Cover photo by Getty Images
Author photo by Bernard Clark

ORCA BOOK PUBLISHERS
PO Box 5626, STN. B
VICTORIA, BC CANADA
V8R 6S4

ORCA BOOK PUBLISHERS
PO Box 468
CUSTER, WA USA
98240-0468

www.orcabook.com
Printed and bound in Canada.

11 10 09 08 • 4 3 2 1

For my parents, Carole and Lucien Lieberman

Acknowledgments

Many people offered advice and feedback during the writing of this novel. I'd like to thank Amanda Dafoe, Tina Grabenhorst, and the other members of my Graduate Writing Workshop at the University of Windsor for their editing suggestions.

Thank you to my Toronto writing group: Elizabeth MacLeod, Dianne Scott, Roswell Spafford, Ania Szado, Elsie Sze and Anne Warrick. Your encouragement, friendship and excellent editing skills are invaluable.

Many thanks to Marcy Lieberman and Louise Friedman for their advice on early drafts of the novel.

A special thanks to Darryl Whetter for his tight editing and for his recommendation that I enter the Orca writing contest.

I am indebted to my agent Pamela Paul for her perseverance and interest in Ellie's life.

I am grateful to both the Ontario Arts Council and the Social Sciences and Humanities Research Council for awarding me grants.

Thanks to Sarah Harvey for fine-tuning my book.

Several people inspired the writing of *Gravity*. Jamie Miller told me about "hitting the high note and staying in the room." Rick Negrin let me know that God is a force just like gravity. Robbie Stocki educated me about Judaism. I owe a special thanks to my brother, Jeff Lieberman, for coming out to me while we were on a walk in an Orthodox Jewish neighborhood in Jerusalem. You got this novel started in my head.

My parents, Carole and Lucien Lieberman, have supported and encouraged both my ongoing interest in Judaism and my writing. I am thankful for their love and support.

And most of all, thank you to my husband, Rob Smith. You keep my feet on the ground and my head in the sky.

One

Neshama shoves an enormous blue duffel bag down the stairs. It slides sloth-like down a few steps and then stops, caught by the wooden banister.

"What, are you leaving forever?" I ask.

"I wish." Neshama smoothes a long blond curl behind her ear and adjusts her fake designer sunglasses on her head.

I snort. "Hard to travel with that bag."

She flaps her shirt away from her stomach. "Will you pleeeese help me?" She smiles, tilting her head to the side.

I sigh and climb up the stairs. Neshama started packing weeks ago, randomly throwing T-shirts, fashion magazines, eyeliner and half a dozen lipsticks into her bag. This morning she was still stuffing romance novels under the bulging zipper.

We each pick up a strap of the duffel bag and half lift, half drag it down the stairs. As we lug the bag into the front hall, I knock my elbow on the newel post; pain shoots up my arm. Neshama tries not to snicker. Even though she's two years older and entering her last year of high school, I'm already four inches taller. That's four more inches of gangly arms, rangy legs, pointy elbows and bony knees.

"That's all you're taking?" She looks at my small red suitcase by the front door.

"It's just going to be Bubbie and me at the cottage."

Our Abba rushes down the stairs behind us with a large canvas suitcase, sweating through his white shirt.

"Ellie, go help your mother, please."

"What's the matter now?"

"Something about her sun hat."

I've already refolded the clothes in Ima's suitcase twice: last night and this morning. Ima has been preparing for months to go to Israel. She made lists: Immodium, film, laundry soap, walking shoes. She went shopping, made neat piles on our dining room table. This morning she is still rearranging her suitcase, randomly sticking things into her bag, wrinkling her blouses, shoving socks and bras into corner pockets.

"Anyway, she needs help. We need to be ready to go before you do." Abba stops. His eyes flicker to Neshama's legs. "Neshama, is that what you're wearing to camp?" He runs his fingers through his curly brown beard.

"Yeah, what's wrong?"

"Your skirt."

Neshama peers over her shoulder at the slit in the back. "It's fine."

Abba frowns. "You can see the back of your knees."

Neshama sighs. "It's hot outside, and everyone wears skirts like this at camp."

"Go and change."

They stand, glaring at each other. I slink up the stairs.

"Ima?" I peer into her dim bedroom. The curtains are drawn, the air conditioner is turned off. Ima sits on the end of her bed, hands slack in her lap, her pointy shoulders hunched. Her open suitcase is a twisted mess of clothes.

"Are you ready to go?"

"I'm not sure."

"Abba says you can't find your hat."

"Oh, I found it." She holds up a crushed straw hat with floppy yellow chrysanthemums on the brim.

"Okay, so can we go then? Bubbie is going to be here any minute." I sit down on the bed next to her, peer at her drawn face, the deep circles under her eyes.

"I'm sure I've forgotten something."

"What?"

"Well, I'm not sure."

"Do you have your toothbrush?"

"Yes."

"Plane ticket? Passport?"

"Abba has those."

"Well, then don't worry. Everything else you can get in Israel."

Abba leans into the room. "Are you coming?" He drums his fingers on the wall, looking at Ima. "Your mother's here."

"I'll be there in a second," Ima says. She turns to me. "Are you sure you're going to be okay with Bubbie for the whole summer?"

"Totally fine. Don't worry." I squeeze Ima's hand and zip up her suitcase, stopping to refold a blouse. Ima sighs as she tucks a chestnut curl under her scarf. She adjusts the belt on her new, long-sleeved sundress and follows me downstairs.

"*Nu*, so are we all ready?" Bubbie says. She pushes an enormous pair of rhinestone-studded sunglasses up her forehead and settles them carefully in her silver hairdo.

Bubbie, Ima's mom, is our country club grandmother. She plays bridge, volunteers for Hadassah and meets friends for golf or tennis twice a week. Today she wears a white polo shirt, beige walking shorts and pink high heels.

"We just have to say *t'fillah ha'derech*," Abba says.

"There's really no time—" Bubbie protests.

"It'll just take a second." Abba whips his prayer book out of his fanny pack and starts chanting the prayer for safe travel, his voice slightly nasal. We stand in the tiny front hall surrounded by luggage. I chant the prayer under my breath. Neshama rolls her eyes. I notice she has changed into a different skirt. Bubbie wiggles her toes, the perfect pale pink ovals of her toenails peeking out of her open-toe pumps.

Abba finishes the prayer, and Ima says, "Amen. Now we sit."

"Oh, c'mon, this is ridiculous," Bubbie says. "You're going to miss your flight."

"Just one minute." Ima ushers us into the living room.

"Ima, the bus is going to leave without me," Neshama wails.

Ima smiles and sits next to Abba on the beige sofa. Neshama, Bubbie and I wait in the doorway.

A moment passes. Ima smiles. "Okay, let's go."

Outside, the sun glares through the thick muggy air. I leave my suitcase on the front porch and help Neshama load her duffel bag into Bubbie's trunk. Abba piles his and Ima's suitcases on top and squishes the lid closed.

"Okay," Bubbie says, "pile in."

Abba hands me a shoebox lined with wax paper. "*Knishes* and *rugelach.*"

"Thanks."

He clumsily smoothes my hair, his wedding ring grazing my forehead. "You'll be careful, right?"

"Yes, Abba."

Ima squeezes my arm and stands on tiptoe to kiss me. "Have a good time at the cottage."

Neshama hugs me. "Don't do anything I wouldn't do."

"I'll be back to pick you up in an hour," Bubbie says. They pull away, waving and smiling.

I walk up the street to drop off my fish tank at my friend Becca's house. When I get back, I sit on the front porch next to my suitcase and stretch out my long legs, wrapping my skinny arms around me. The humidity makes my straight hair flip out at the ends. A sticky layer of sweat forms between my almost touching thighs.

My red vinyl suitcase holds two skirts—one khaki, one denim—a saggy one-piece bathing suit, seven pairs of cotton briefs, two beige A-cup bras, a rain slicker, my old gray sweater and five pastel T-shirts with three-quarter-length sleeves in mauve, peach, baby blue, yellow and mint green. In the outside compartment are books (*Encyclopedia of the Ocean*; *Linnaeus: The Man and His Work*; *Frogs of Ontario*), binoculars, one Hello Kitty notebook, six HB #2 pencils, three ballpoint pens, a magnifying glass and my *Complete Artscroll Siddur*. I've been ready to go for weeks.

I can hear endless cars and trucks whizzing by on Eglinton Avenue. Weeds push up through the walkway to our house; a small spindly tree wilts on our square plot of lawn. The heat rises thick and squalid with Toronto summer pollution. I get up and step into the shade of the front porch and settle into an old tan wicker chair, picking at the loose strands on the armrest. Only one more hour, and I'm done with the city for the summer.

I'm leaving asphalt, concrete and traffic. I'm leaving polyester school skirts stained with sweat from sitting on vinyl seats. It's the summer of 1987. I'm fifteen and I'm leaving Torah and *Mishna* classes for trees, the lake and the blue blue sky.

When Bubbie pulls up in her white Cadillac an hour later, she rolls down the window and leans her head out. "Are you ready, kid?" I nod and she releases the trunk. "Let's blow this pop stand."

I drop my bag in the car and hop into the icy cool, beige and maroon leather interior.

Two hours of traffic: stalls on the 401, rubberneckers in minivans, pickup trucks with ATVs, old Volkswagens carrying fancy canoes. Exhaust shimmers in the heat off the asphalt. Off the collector lanes, then back on. Bottleneck at Pickering. An old Mustang full of teenage boys snakes up the center shoulder, BMWs politely honking. We pass mini malls edged against Lake Ontario, industrial areas, the occasional rolling hill. Bubbie sings along to the Supremes. *Can't help myself. I love you and nobody else.*

Finally we turn off the 401, and there are just trees and rocks and bushes, the occasional marsh, black stumps growing up through the water like prehistoric remnants of forest. I want to roll down the window and let the fresh air blow my hair back, but I know Bubbie will complain about the wind on her neck.

I twist sideways in my seat and lean against the door. A smile sneaks across my lips.

"Do you think it'll be warm enough to swim?" I ask.

"Of course. I bought you a suit. I wasn't sure if you had one."

"Oh, thank you."

Bubbie sighs. "You don't have one?"

"No, I have one. It's just plain black."

"We're almost at the turnoff. Do you want to stop for something to eat?"

"Uh, no, thanks."

"You're not hungry?"

"No, not really."

"Not even for French fries?" Bubbie makes a face.

"They're probably not kosher."

"What about a salad?"

"Bubbie, the whole restaurant wouldn't be kosher."

She shakes her head and pats my shoulder. "If that's what you want."

Bubbie has packed an entire store of kosher food for me: jars of pickles, smoked meat, loaves of rye bread, cream cheese, tubs of coleslaw, hummus, fresh pasta that we will have to eat by the end of the week. She promised she'd prepare only kosher food.

BUBBIE FINALLY TURNS off the highway and maneuvers her old Cadillac slowly down a gravel lane. I roll down the window to hang out my head. Frogs chirp in the marsh. I see water by the edge of the forest, or is it the other way round?

I am out of the car before Bubbie even turns off the motor. "Come and see how nice the cottage is," she calls.

"Later," I yell over my shoulder. I run down the winding gravel path past the wooden cottage, out of the darkness of the fir trees, across the grass to the shore. Water shimmers in the late afternoon light, lapping against the giant slabs of rock. A cool breeze ruffles the surface, blowing my sticky hair off my face. I reach the end of the dock, sit for a second; then I lie down. The crickets sing. I inhale the scent of lake, letting my limbs ease into the rough wood of the dock, dangling my hands in the fresh cool water.

WHEN I WAKE early the next morning, I can see slow heavy mist twisting over the glassy surface of the water. I slip out of my sheets and quietly pad across the living room floor so as not to wake Bubbie. Outside, I make my way across the porch, down the stairs, through the dewy grass and past the hammock hanging between two maple trees. I sit on the dock, shivering in my sweater. I pull my knees into my chest, the dock cold under my bare feet. Across the bay the island is obscured by the thick mist. To my left, sun slants over the marsh of tree stumps and cattails. Out in the bay beyond the point, a family of loons slowly disappear into the thick vapor.

Bubbie rents this cottage every summer, but the first and only other time I've been here I was seven. I'd never seen a lake, a forest, or wildflowers, had never left the city. We arrived in the evening, our bodies stuck to the hot plastic car seats, the metal seatbelts burning our skin. When we pulled off the highway onto the gravel road down to the cottage there was a sudden cool breeze through the deep green of the trees. Abba parked the car by the woodpile, and Bubbie came down to meet us. It was twilight; the first stars were appearing in the pinkish sky.

"Come," Bubbie had said to Neshama and me. She took us down to the water's edge and we waded in beside the dock. I nudged small snail shells with my toes. The island across the bay was covered with pines, the occasional birch gleaming white. "I've never seen so many trees!" I exclaimed.

"Or mosquitoes," Neshama added.

"Can we go swimming?"

"Sure, I'll come with you." Bubbie stripped off her sundress, and waded in naked. Ima and Abba had gone into the cottage to unpack. Neshama and I looked at each other, giggled and took off our clothes. We eased our naked bodies into the water, our toes sliding into the viscous mud, darkness enveloping us, washing away the city. I fell in love with the wet cool on my hot skin.

I floated on my back, looking up at the sky, listening to the waves slap against the shore. The stars glimmered like a mosaic of lights, brighter than I'd ever seen before.

Abba was furious when he came down to the water and saw us wrapped in just our towels. "You have bathing suits. Why aren't you wearing them!"

"Oh, who cares?" Bubbie said to him. "They're just little girls. No one is around."

"And you?"

Bubbie wrapped the towel around herself tighter. "So, don't look."

"When *Moshiach* comes, there'll be time for swimming naked."

"Would you just relax and forget about your religious *mishigas* for a day? Enough waiting."

Ima said nothing. She just sat tight-lipped on the porch, sweating in her long-sleeved blouse.

Abba packed us off in a hurry.

I have been waiting to come back ever since. I have been waiting for a breeze through the pine trees on a hot summer afternoon and the chorus of peeping frogs mating in the swamp.

Waiting is in my blood. My parents are professionals at it. After years of planning, they are finally in Israel for the summer. Only Bubbie waits for no one and no thing. Life is to live now. To enjoy. "What?" Bubbie says. "I should sit and wait for the messiah to come?"

I stand up on the end of the dock with my prayer book and sing "*Shma Yisroel Adonai Eloheinu, Adonai Echad.*"

Hear O Israel, the Lord is our God, the Lord is One. My voice echoes across the water.

I have been waiting to pray outside. In Toronto, surrounded by paved streets, it seems silly to pray for rain for the crops. Once I sneaked out to pray in the ravine, but people kept coming by, and I didn't sing out loud.

I chant, *"Ve'ahafatah, adonai."* Love the Lord.

The screen door slams. Bubbie comes out wearing a long, faded blue T-shirt, her legs bare. She strides down to the dock and sheds the T-shirt, revealing a saggy pink swimsuit. "Take me to the river, wash me down," she bellows before she dives into the water. The mist has lifted, and the sky and water are cerulean. I close my prayer book and watch Bubbie's arms scissor powerfully through the water in even strokes. She swims out to the middle of the bay until I can barely see her, just the white of her hair. She waves to me, then swims out of sight. I try to continue my prayers. I keep glancing up anxiously until she comes back.

Bubbie's stroke propels her through the water, her arms rotating in an even rhythm. She swims up to the ladder, her breath deep and heavy. Pulling herself onto the dock, her arm muscles flex underneath her wrinkled skin.

"I didn't know you could do that."

Bubbie wipes water from her face with her towel. "You mean swim?"

"Yeah."

"You know I go to the club all the time."

I shrug. "I thought you did water aerobics or something."

She laughs. "What made you think that?"

"I don't know."

Bubbie towels off her hair and bathing suit.

"I've never seen that suit before."

She shrugs. "I only wear it here. Are you going in?"

I shake my head and sigh. "I wish I could swim like you."

"I'll teach you."

"Really?"

"We'll be here a month. What else are you going to do?" She plucks at her bathing suit straps. "Besides, it's important to stay in shape. All those rabbis with their *bochels* and high cholesterol. I'd be happy to help you improve your stroke."

Neshama is always going on about exercise too. She and Ima both have tiny bird bodies. Ima really does look like a small white sparrow, her backbones poking through her skin. Neshama works out. Lifts weights. Abba's always bugging her about what she wears at the gym. Neshama says she wears track pants and a T-shirt, but I've seen exercise tights when she does her wash.

Neshama has a tight little bum and stomach muscles that she can clench together in a hard ribbon down her belly when she leans forward and grunts.

Bubbie heads back up to the cottage, and I follow behind her, even though I'm not finished my prayers. The sun beats down, and my stomach feels empty.

The cottage is a dark log cabin with a screened-in porch. The kitchen has open shelves instead of cupboards, and an old stainless steel sink. In the main room a large stone fireplace dominates the far wall. Several old orange recliners and a reddish brown couch droop in the center of the room.

A stack of *Life* magazines from the seventies fills a wooden crate beside the couch. An old lantern and a pair of cross-country skis hang above the fireplace.

Bubbie pours herself a cup of coffee and grabs a Popsicle stick from a package in a drawer.

"Coffee?" she offers.

"No, thanks."

"Popsicle stick?"

"Pardon?"

"Just kidding." She brandishes the Popsicle stick at me. "They're so I don't smoke." She pops the stick in her mouth and chews with her back teeth. "I will not smoke today." Her hair is flat on one side, her eyelids bare of eye shadow or liner. I have never seen her without makeup.

"Bubbie, you quit smoking five years ago."

"Yes, but now I'm stuck on the sticks." She puts bread in the toaster.

I watch Bubbie chew. "So, what do you do here?"

Bubbie runs her hands through her hair, rests a hip against the counter. "Swim in the morning, read in the afternoon, obsess over birds. Yellow finch." She points out over the porch to the bird feeder.

"You know about birds?"

Bubbie nods. "What are you going to do this summer?"

I sip my orange juice and look out the sliding glass doors. "I don't know. Look for frogs, practice swimming."

Bubbie hands me a piece of toast. I get out the peanut butter and smooth it on. I quickly whisper a blessing before taking a bite.

"You know, you don't have to do that here."

"The *brucha*?"

"Yeah, I'm not going to report you."

I shrug. "It's just habit."

"Is that why do you do it?"

I take a bite of toast. "Yeah, and you know, to be closer to *Hashem*."

Bubbie chokes on her coffee. "God?"

"Yeah, God."

"And what do you think that is?"

I pause mid-bite, my brow crinkling. "*Hashem*? You know, God is just God. Creator, commandments, all that stuff."

Bubbie gawks at me. "You really believe all that?"

"What's not to believe?"

I give Bubbie a fuzzy answer because I don't really spend much time thinking about God. Keeping kosher and saying prayers is just normal to me. Bubbie has me confused with Ima and Abba, who are reborn Jews. Every ritual they keep is about "loving God" and "being spiritual."

God is too big an idea to even hold in my head all at one time, vaporous and, well, enormous. It's like trying to think about the whole ocean all at once. I can only focus on one mollusk or seaweed tendril at a time.

AFTER BREAKFAST BUBBIE gives me the new bathing suit, a blue two-piece. "A bikini?" I say incredulously.

"It's not a bikini. It's two pieces, tank style. I thought you'd be too long in the body for a one-piece."

I stare at it.

In the bedroom I pull on the suit, trying to see myself in the small mirror above the wooden bureau. I trace my fingers over the scooped neckline. The bottoms are cut low over the belly and high over my narrow hips. I lift my arms over my head, striking a pose in front of the mirror.

Down on the dock a gentle breeze laps the water into small waves. I hang onto the ladder, trying to keep my feet out of the weeds.

Bubbie stands on the dock bent at the waist, arms rotating. "You need to cup the water with your hands and pull back. Two motions: cup and pull."

I stand in the muck, circling my arms.

"Good. Now kick your feet at the same time."

"Now?"

"Sure."

I take a deep breath and plunge into the dark water. My arms crash over my head: cup and pull. I gasp for air, hold it, drag the other arm up and over. Feet: kick. Hands: cup and pull. I forget to breathe. Water rushes up my nose. I surface spitting and coughing, trying to keep my feet out of the jelly-like sand.

"Good," Bubbie sings out from her deck chair. "Good try."

I practice again and again until I am blue and shivering. "Enough," Bubbie says. "Enough for today." She passes me a towel, and I collapse into a deck chair.

"Look at those chicken arms."

"What?"

Bubbie pokes my upper arm. "Chicken arms. You need muscles to swim."

I examine my bony arms.

"You should do push-ups, every day. Then you'll be cutting through that water like a fish."

Bubbie goes up for drinks. I get down on my chest and try to push my body up. I grunt, but nothing moves. I roll up my towel under my legs and try pushing up from my knees.

"Keep your butt down, back flat." Bubbie puts a glass of lemonade down on the dock for me.

I try again, face burning, heart pounding.

"That's better. You'll look like Charles Atlas in no time."

Whoever that is. I collapse onto my belly and peer at the dark green shadows the wooden slats of the dock throw onto the water.

Bubbie picks up a biography of Henry Kissinger, the brim of her floppy straw hat shading her face. I drop my head back, let the heat seep into me. I too will dive and swim all the way across the bay.

FRIDAY AFTERNOON I pull out a set of small candleholders and a bottle of kosher wine from the box Abba packed for me. "It's *Shabbos*," I announce to Bubbie.

"Well, what do you know. I lose track of the days up here." Bubbie opens the freezer and tosses a bag of *challah* buns at me. I catch the bag and take out two to defrost. A few frozen poppy seeds flake off.

If we were at home there'd be a special meal—chicken or salmon fillets—and a white tablecloth. Tonight we're only having pasta salad and corn-on-the-cob on the picnic table outside.

When it's time to sit down to dinner, the sun just starting to descend, Bubbie says, "Okay, let's do those blessings."

I stand up reluctantly and whisper the blessing. I've never blessed the *Shabbos* candles without Ima and Neshama singing beside me. Bubbie watches me, not joining in, her arms crossed against her chest.

"Are you done?" she asks when I stop praying.

"You're supposed to say amen."

"Amen." She goes to get the corn before I can bless the wine or the cold rocks of bread.

If Ima and Abba were here we'd sing a song before dinner. Abba would bless me, laying his hands on my head and telling me he hoped I'd turn out like Sarah, Rachel, Rebecca and Leah. Neshama and I would harmonize *zemirot* after dinner, and there'd be Abba's apple cake or *rugelach* for dessert.

Bubbie turns on the radio while I'm still chanting the prayer after meals. I glare at her and leave her to finish the cleaning up by herself. Down on the dock I slap a few mosquitoes, then I decide to go up to bed.

I say good night to Bubbie as I pass her in the living room.

"Sleep well," she says.

In my dark room, I extend my arms, feeling for the bed. I bump my knee against the bed frame.

"Are you all right in there?" Bubbie asks from the living room.

"Fine."

"Do you want me to come in and turn on the light?"

"No, thanks."

"Can I do it anyway?"

"No, that's okay." I climb into bed.

Bubbie sighs. "I'll get you a night-light for next week."

"Oh, good idea."

I don't turn the lights on because *Shabbos*, the Sabbath, is a day of rest. All work is forbidden, including driving, cooking and lighting fires. Observant Jews don't turn lights on and off or use the phone or radio because using electricity is like lighting a fire. We even unscrew the light bulb in the fridge so the light doesn't turn on every time you open it. We pre-tear the toilet paper because even ripping is a form of work.

Bubbie thinks this is totally crazy. Neshama also thinks it nuts and has refused to leave the lights alone for ages. She even re-screws the light bulb in the fridge. Ima and Abba just ignore her.

I like not using electricity on *Shabbos*. It's not that I think flipping a switch is work, I just like the different feeling. The weekday rush isn't followed by weekend chaos, but by stillness and calm. No radio or TV, not even any cooking. Each restriction or change reminds me that it is good to rest. At home we have light timers, so it's not like we're stumbling around in the dark.

In the living room I hear Bubbie playing with the radio and then finally turning it off. She flicks off the lights and the sliver of yellow beneath my door vanishes. I turn over in bed and let the quiet of *Shabbos* fill the room.

TWO

I get down in the weeds to watch a small green frog tremble at the edge of the water. Dew soaks through my T-shirt, causing goose bumps to form up my legs. The frog croaks high and light, not soft like the peepers, or throaty like the bullfrog. I edge closer, slowly, shivering in the damp grass, legs tangled in wet skirt. The frog has shiny webbed feet, no definitive spots or stripes, probably *rama clamitans*. I lie still, watching its tongue dart out; then I reach out, tentative, hesitating. It jumps away, scared by my approaching hands.

Linnaeus looked at nature, and where others saw chaos, he saw order. Clear lines, hierarchies of phylum, class, all the way down to individual species. Taxonomy. God's creations in neat sets. Judaism is a lot like taxonomy, even if Bubbie and Neshama think it's only oppression and patriarchy. It's also beauty and concision and order. There's a rule or law for just about everything, an order or right way to do things, from how to get married, to how to put on your shoes. Give me any week, and I can tell you what Torah portion you're supposed to read, what lesson you should learn.

Bubbie keeps asking me if I'm bored. I'm not, not for a moment. She shakes her head and wonders aloud how many teenage girls want to spend all day alone or hang out with their grandmothers. I just tell her I'm busy. And I am. For the past two weeks, I've prayed each morning in the trees behind the cottage. I mumble through the prayers quickly, my voice muffled by the branches. My voice sounds thin and lonely without the other girls from school or the *shul* congregation. I rush through without thinking about the words. After breakfast I practice swimming with Bubbie, splashing around, trying to keep water out of my nose and mouth. The rest of the time, I only want to sit and watch and, even more, to listen. I never knew nature was so noisy. The sun heats up, the dew evaporates, and a chorus of croaking frogs, chattering squirrels, squawking ducks and wind-rattled leaves fills the air. Fish gurgle and make small splashes on the lake; the waves lap against the dock. The longer I sit, the more I hear.

I wade farther into the snarled weeds, water creeping up my skirt and into my bathing suit when I crouch down. Thick mud squishes between my toes. The frog's eyes move, its cheeks pulsing. I cup my hands, anticipating the webbed feet against my palms.

"Hey," a voice calls out across the water.

I startle, jerking upright. The frog hops into the weeds. A girl approaches in a canoe. I haven't seen anyone else up here except when we go for groceries in Northbrook.

The girl calls out across the water, "Hey, where's Craig?"

I stand up. My skirt sticks to my legs. "Who?" Shading my eyes, I climb onto the dock. The girl paddles over.

She has long blond hair twisted into two loose braids down her back. She is wearing jean shorts and her tank top reveals fair-skinned, freckled shoulders.

"Hi." I wipe mud off my hands onto my skirt.

"Is Craig here?" she asks, pulling up alongside the dock.

"Craig?"

"This is his cottage."

"My grandmother rented it this month—"

"Oh." She gazes across the bay.

"Um, is that your own canoe?" I admire the glossy red shell, the wood interior.

"Yeah," she says, distracted. "How long are you staying?"

I sit down at the end of the dock. "Until the end of August. I'm Ellie."

"Lindsay." She tosses her hair and looks me up and down. "What were you trying to do over there?"

"I was…well, I saw this frog. I was trying to catch it."

"Catch a frog?"

"Yeah, I wanted to see what kind it was. I couldn't tell without picking it up."

She laughs. "You're kidding, right?"

I don't say anything.

"Are you into science or something?"

I shrug. A pair of loons surfaces, their white necklaces distracting me. "I didn't know there were other people around," I say, staring past her at the birds.

"Yeah, down the bend." Lindsay points over her shoulder.

I rinse my feet in the cool lake water. "So what do you and Craig do here?"

"Hang out. Fish." She twirls her paddle in her hands.

There's a pole I keep eyeing in the basement of the cottage, but Bubbie says she doesn't know how to use it. "I'd like to go fishing," I blurt. "There's a pole and all, but I don't know how…"

Lindsay grabs hold of the dock. "You just cast and reel in. I suppose I could show you."

I lean forward. "Really? That would be great."

Lindsay looks up from her paddle. "Well, whenever." She reaches out to push away from the dock. "See you then."

"Wait." I stand up.

"What?"

"Well, if you have some time later, maybe you could…"

Lindsay sighs. "I suppose we could go for a paddle now. I don't have my pole."

I smile. "I'll be back in a moment." I try to walk slowly up to the cottage for a life jacket and paddle.

When I come back down to the water, Lindsay is standing in the middle of the canoe, floating a few feet from the dock. She looks at me and grins. "Watch this."

She leans over and balances her hands and then her feet on the gunwales. I watch, fascinated, as she raises herself to a crouch. She's stripped off her tank top and jean shorts to reveal just three small patches of white fabric held together with string. All the girls I know dress modestly; even their swimsuits are like my plain old one.

Lindsay's breasts hang full and pendulous in the cups, her hips naked except for the little ties. She slowly stands up, thigh muscles flexing, arms outstretched, eyes focused.

When she is fully upright, she breaks into a smile and gives her hips a slight toss, rocking the boat. "Now watch."

As if I could take my eyes off her. I squint into the sun and hold my breath, staring in amazement as she bends her knees and lifts her arms. She swings them down and hurls her body into the water beside the canoe. The canoe heaves wildly and flips over, and Lindsay lands with an impressive splash. She surfaces, her hair slick against her skull.

"Neat, eh? I'm trying to do it without flipping the canoe."

I nod. She didn't even check the depth first.

"Wanna try?"

"Neh."

"Oh, come on, it's fun."

"Maybe later."

Lindsay shrugs and dives toward the canoe.

I couldn't possibly do that. Besides not being a good swimmer, I have lousy balance. If I actually could screw up the courage to jump, I'd probably bump my head on the boat. And I could never parade around wearing so little.

Lindsay grabs hold of the canoe and kicks it back toward the shore. "So how old are you anyway?"

I zip up my life jacket. "Fifteen."

She stands in the water and flips the canoe. Her nipples, pointy and brown, show through the white material of her bathing suit. My stomach tightens into a knot. "I thought you were younger," she says.

Even though I'm already five-foot-eight, I still get mistaken for twelve. "How old are you?"

"Same." Lindsay glances up at me. "Don't you want to change into shorts or a bathing suit or something?"

I shake my head and roll up my skirt at the waist a few times.

Lindsay steadies the wobbling canoe as I step into the bow. "Keep your body low," she instructs. She expertly jumps in and pushes us away from the dock. I kneel like Lindsay does, and plunge my paddle into the water, crushing my fingers against the side of the boat. I draw in my breath.

"Have you never been in a canoe before?"

"Ah, not really." I turn around and smile at her.

She rolls her eyes. "Okay, put one hand at the top of the paddle and the other lower down. Draw it through the water, like this."

I try again, splashing myself. Even so, the canoe edges forward.

We head out into the bay. I can see gulls bobbing in the protected water of Horseshoe Island. The wind picks up and the canoe rocks underneath me, small waves slapping against the sides. My arms tire and my back gets sore, but I keep paddling. When we get to the middle of the bay, Lindsay leans back in the boat, and using her lifejacket as a pillow, tips her face up to the sun. I flip my legs around to face the center of the canoe, watching the blue ripples all around. I imagine paddling along the shore and not coming back to the cottage. I know some lakes eventually lead to salt water, to throbbing jellyfish, purple and orange sea stars, rubbery sea cucumbers.

GRAVITY

"You're not *that* bad for someone who has never been in a canoe," Lindsay admits.

"Thanks."

Lindsay undoes her braids, releasing her long, dark blond hair. The wind tosses it across her face, rippled strands catching on her bikini straps.

My own brown hair is always limp. Even when I blow-dry it with my head upside down and brush furiously, it's greasy and lifeless within twenty minutes. I drift my hand in the cool water and close my eyes. Her hair would be silky between my fingers. I flick open my eyes.

On the way back Lindsay asks, "So, how come you've never been in a boat before?"

"I just never was. I'm from Toronto."

"Didn't you ever go to camp or a cottage?"

"Just day camp. In the city."

"Only swimming pools?"

"Sort of." I think of the girls' turn to go in the water, all those shrieking voices. "My sister's working at a camp."

"Yeah? How come you didn't go?"

"It's an all girls' camp—not my thing," I tell her, trying to sound cool. That's not the real reason. I wanted to come here, to see the lake.

"Only girls? That would suck." She pushes her rippled hair out of her face and tucks it under her bikini strap.

We head toward the dock, the wind pushing us from behind. I don't splash once.

Lindsay maneuvers us back up to the dock, grabs hold of the edge. "So I'll see you around."

· 25 ·

"If you have some time, you know, maybe, you could show me how to cast."

"Yeah, maybe sometime." Lindsay looks down at the boat.

I climb out of the canoe, my foot catching on the edge of my skirt. "Okay," I say after I untangle myself. "Bye then."

As Lindsay paddles away, a shiver travels from my neck down through my body and exits out my knees.

"DO YOU WANT to go for a walk?"

"I think I'll stay behind."

Bubbie shrugs and grabs her droopy straw hat.

I flop down in the hammock with my book about the sea and try to read about the lifecycle of a periwinkle. I keep glancing over the water.

It's been three days since Lindsay came by. I'm no longer fascinated by my nature guides or *Linnaeus: The Man and His Work*. I can't concentrate. I've studied the frogs, identified trees, watched the sunfish from the dock, the cardinals, blue jays and hummingbirds from the hammock. I've gawked at the loons, the occasional merganser and blue heron. I've caught moths, swatted black flies, horseflies and mosquitoes. I've watched the squirrels try to raid the bird feeder, and even though I saw a deer in the trees, I'm bored.

"Do you wanna go check out the mini-golf?" Bubbie asks when she gets back.

"Neh."

"What's with you?" Bubbie leans against the maple tree, gives the hammock a push.

"Nothing."

Bubbie smirks.

I sigh. "I was hoping that girl down the lake would take me fishing."

"So walk over there," Bubbie says, exasperated.

"I thought you could only go by boat."

Bubbie points to the trail leading off through the woods. "Just follow it past the campground and you'll come to their cottage. It's a huge A-frame with skylights—brand new—you can't miss it. More like a chalet than a cottage," Bubbie sniffs.

I head over in the afternoon, following the trail through the woods. I pass a swamp, where a dumped car's rusted metal frame is slowly yielding to the elements, and enter an area of low-lying sumac bushes. The forest opens up to reveal a manicured stretch of lawn, an elegant house on a hill. A new dock juts out over the water, a chaise longue and glass table angled to catch the sun. Sliding glass doors and tall windows stretch across the front of the cottage, revealing long fans turning in a row across the open front room.

A woman wearing a red bikini with her fingernails painted the same crimson shade talks on the phone on the porch. Small cups of material cover her full breasts; a thin strip of fabric snakes between her bum cheeks.

I tentatively climb the stairs.

"I *know* it's for safety," she says, "but I don't want rails on *my* balcony." She mouths "Lindsay?" at me. I nod, and she waves me inside the house.

"I don't *have* dogs or small children," she continues. "If I have to put rails up, I'm going to hire you to take them down the second the place is inspected."

The screen door slides smoothly open and glides closed behind me. Lindsay rocks back and forth in a recliner, bare legs tucked inside a baggy M.A.S.H. T-shirt, a blue baseball cap pulled low over her forehead.

She looks up. "I need to read one more page. Lady Eliza is just about to make out with Sir Reginald." She holds up a Harlequin romance. The couple on the cover embrace wildly, the woman's breasts threatening to spill out of her low-cut dress, hair cascading through the man's hands.

Lindsay's cottage is like a magazine picture. Sun slants down from the skylights across a wooden coffee table and richly upholstered, deep red chairs. Across from the chairs is a green leather couch. I perch on the armrest and look out over my shoulder at the lake. A hutch behind Lindsay by the bedroom doors holds wineglasses and several bottles of wine.

Lindsay puts down her book and stuffs a few peanuts in her mouth from a small glass bowl. "So?"

"I was hoping you might come by again."

"I've been pretty busy."

"Oh, with your mom?" I instantly regret the words.

Lindsay giggles. "Yeah right, with my mom. We read trash together."

I tap my sandal on the pine floors. "I thought maybe we'd go fishing or something."

"Something? Like play with frogs?" she teases.

An angry blush climbs over my cheeks. "Just forget it," I mumble. I smooth my skirt over my legs and head for the door.

"Wait."

I turn around. "What?"

"You don't need to leave yet. I could show you my stripper routine."

"Your what?" I stop by the door.

Lindsay takes off her cap, her hair falling over her shoulders. "Let me show you." She stands up and struts across the room, hips swinging, her mouth slightly open in a sexy pout. She stops in front of me and gyrates her hips down to the floor, bending her knees open wide. She twists her T-shirt up at the waist to expose her taut belly, her head tipping back to bare her white neck.

I freeze by the door, bug-eyed.

"Wanna try?"

I back against the wall. My body doesn't move that way. "I couldn't—"

Lindsay eyes my baggy skirt. "How about just the walk?" She struts, one leg in front of the other, swinging a hip to the side. "And a one and two and turn." She swivels on the ball of her foot, hair fanning out. "Now you try."

"I can't." I clutch my blushing cheeks.

"Well, have you ever tried this?" Lindsay grabs an empty plastic tumbler off the coffee table. "Watch," she instructs. She holds the glass in both hands and slowly draws her tongue up the plastic, flicking it over the rim. "That's called the butterfly flick. I read about it in my mom's *Cosmo:* 'Five Tips To A Better Blow Job'."

I stare, my mouth open. My hands twist behind my back.

"It's better on a beer bottle, of course." Lindsay holds out the glass.

I shake my head, eyes wide. Lindsay shrugs. She closes her eyes, leans her head back, and starts at the base of the glass again. She gives a fake groan, then collapses back in the chair, giggling. Her T-shirt has slipped off her freckled shoulder. I stare at the curve of the top of her breasts.

I tug nervously at my fingers, cracking my knuckles. "My parents don't really read magazines," I tell her. "My dad, he's into Talmud, that's Jewish law. He's in this club called the *Daf Yomi*, which means he reads a whole page of Talmud every day." Shut up, Ellie. "They'll be finished after the year two thousand. There'll be this huge party in New York for it." I'm talking too fast and Lindsay is staring at me, a bemused expression on her face.

She swivels her tongue around the rim and then holds out the glass. "Wanna try? It's a good skill to have."

I shudder. "No, that's okay."

"I think I'd like to be a stripper when I grow up, so it's important to know how to do these things," she explains.

"You mean take your clothes off in public?" I bunch my skirt in my hands.

"Yeah, and get paid for it too. How *easy*. I'll either do that or be a lawyer like my mom."

"Those are pretty different jobs."

"Yeah, I think I'd rather be a stripper." Lindsay sits, tucking her feet underneath her. She holds up the glass. "Guys love this."

I swallow. "Have you done it?"

Lindsay winks and giggles. "Not yet. I like to keep in shape though, just in case." She leans closer to me. "I dare you. I double dog dare you." Her eyes flash.

"I should get going," I say. "My grandmother is probably waiting for me to eat lunch. We'll be having this soup, borscht. It's made from beets."

Lindsay sighs, starts to stand up and flops back in the easy chair. She swivels side to side, pushing off the coffee table with her feet. "Fine. Go home."

"Okay, so maybe I'll see you later."

"Whatever."

She picks up the Harlequin and absently scratches her chin.

I stare at her exposed shoulder, the green T-shirt setting off the curved muscle. My stomach contracts into a tight ball.

"I'll do it." I grab a thick goblet from the wine rack on the hutch by the bedroom doors and draw my tongue up the stem, flick it over the rim. A layer of dust coats my tongue. I bang the wineglass back on the hutch. "See you later."

I catch a glimpse of Lindsay's surprised face as I run down the porch steps.

I run along the path back to our cottage and head straight to the dock. I strip off my khaki skirt and peach T-shirt and jump into the water wearing my new bathing suit. Water shoots up my nose, but I swim all the way to the raft, arms flailing, gasping as I grab the ladder. Bubbie waves wildly and claps from the porch. "Good for you, I knew you could do it," she hollers. I wave back weakly.

I practice diving off the raft over and over, hurtling myself into the water until I can stand and swing my arms over my head, propelling myself as gracefully as a dolphin.

THE NEXT MORNING I lie in the hammock watching a squirrel scamper up the maple tree. It runs down a branch and leaps onto the top of the bird feeder. Chickadees and cardinals flutter away. The squirrel's claws scrape furiously on the green plastic, sliding over the edge to the ground. The feeder swings wildly. I turn over in the hammock, and the squirrel darts away.

I hear splashing down at the dock. I roll over and prop up my head. Lindsay hauls a fishing rod and tackle out of her canoe. I pretend not to see her.

She wears a tank top over a black bathing suit, her hair in a tight ponytail at the base of her neck. Long strands drift around her head when she walks toward me.

"Hi," she says.

I don't move. "Hi."

Lindsay puts down the tackle box, props the rod against a tree. "I thought we'd go fishing."

"No, thanks."

"Oh, come on." Lindsay leans one hip against the rope of the hammock, making it swing.

I take a big breath. "I thought you'd have better things to do." Like strip.

Lindsay doesn't say anything for a moment. She slaps a mosquito away from her shoulder. Finally she says, "My mom's boyfriend just came."

"So?"

Lindsay shrugs. "He's gross."

I flip back over. "How?"

"He's creepy and annoying."

"Really?" I flip my legs sideways in the hammock to face Lindsay. "How long is he staying?"

She sighs and leans against the maple tree. "Until we leave, or hopefully only until his fax situation becomes urgent. Then he'll have to drive at least to Kingston."

"Why don't you like him?"

"He's greasy and way younger than my mom. He'll be gone in a month or so. There'll be some other sleazy guy after that. Anyway, I brought you some clothes." Lindsay pulls a pair of jean shorts and a tank top out of a plastic shopping bag. "Here, you can have these."

I get out of the hammock and hold up the clothes. "What for?"

"To wear, stupid." She punches me on the arm. "They're too small for me."

"Are you sure?"

Lindsay cracks her gum. "I can't get the waist done up anymore."

I hesitate, looking at the clothes. I have always wanted to wear shorts in the summer, instead of my baggy skirt, but I can't imagine my naked thighs or bare shoulders.

"Are you sure you don't need these anymore?"

Lindsay nods. "Are you changing or what?"

I stare at Lindsay's enormous blueish green eyes. She returns my gaze without flinching.

Lindsay follows me up to the cottage. I scoot into the bedroom to change, try to get the door closed before she comes in, but she plunks herself down on the patchwork bedspread and picks *Linnaeus* off the night table. I wedge myself beside the only piece of furniture, the pine chest with the cranberry glass lamp, and pull on the shorts before taking off my skirt. The denim cutoffs rest loosely on my hips. I stare down at my slightly hairy, bare pale legs.

"Aren't you going to put on the top?" she asks.

I look at it laid out on the bed. "I...I might burn."

"Sunblock."

"I haven't shaved."

"Who cares, it's a cottage."

I turn around, take a breath, yank off my T-shirt and pull on the tank top. Ellie, you could have just said, *I don't wear tank tops.*

"There, that's better," Lindsay says, popping a bubble. "You can't fish in a skirt. Well, you can, but it's weird."

The tank top is thick white cotton. It's plain, fitted, a little faded. I feel naked.

"What does your necklace say?" Lindsay comes up close to me. I can smell the peppermint of her gum, the soapy smell of shampoo.

I gulp. "Oh, it's Hebrew."

Lindsay lifts the Star of David off my skin, peers at it closely. "What does the writing mean?"

"It says Zion, love for Israel."

Lindsay drops the charm. Her fingers graze my collarbone, my skin tingling.

"I wish I had long legs like yours," she says.

"Too skinny," I say, tucking one leg behind the other.

Lindsay is tall, yet not lanky like me. She has muscular legs. Saturday morning soccer, I bet.

Down on the dock Lindsay shows me how to hold the rod. I want to cast from the canoe. Lindsay laughs. "Practice on land first, or we'll tip." She scratches a mosquito bite on her leg. "How come you don't know how to cast?"

"I told you, I've never been to a cottage before." I practice releasing and reeling in the line.

"Well, what *do* you know?"

I cast my line, the hook forming a huge arc before sinking out in the bay. "That was beautiful, wasn't it?" I say over my shoulder.

Lindsay nods. "It was." She sits on the dock, her feet dangling in the water.

"I know all about the sea, except I haven't been yet." I reel in the line, place the rod over my shoulder and flick it over my head, releasing the catch. The hook whizzes out into the water. "I went to Niagara Falls last summer, to Marine Land. I held a starfish in my hand."

Lindsay stares at me. I hold my gaze steady. "The starfish was wet and brittle, and I could see hundreds of its tiny feelers moving, feel them clinging to my skin." The whole time I'm rambling, I can't take my eyes off Lindsay's hip, the jut of her bone above the waist of her shorts. "The sea star clung to my skin," I repeat.

"You are *so* weird."

I feel myself blush from my chin to just below my eyes.

"I also know all about Houdini from my sister. Did you know he could even escape the Russian police? He jumped off the Detroit Bridge in a water can and escaped. He could hold his breath forever."

Lindsay stands up. "You're getting weirder." She flashes me a smile. "Is your whole family like this?"

"Don't even ask."

WHEN I GET back to the cottage Bubbie is drinking a gin and tonic on the porch.

"Lindsay asked me to her house for dinner."

Bubbie eyes my outfit. "So? You didn't want to go?"

"I didn't know what they'd serve."

Bubbie laughs and squeezes my arm. "You could just tell them you're kosher or vegetarian."

"I told them you were expecting me." I grab a chip from the plastic bowl.

Bubbie nods, and I help her bring out food to the picnic table: smoked meat sandwiches and potato salad made with vinegar dressing, the way I like it.

After dinner we sit on the dock, slapping at mosquitoes. Bubbie slides into an Adirondack chair and lights a cigarette.

"I thought you quit."

"I occasionally like to shove one more nail in my coffin."

"What happened to the Popsicle sticks?"

"I cheat every once in awhile." Bubbie looks at my legs. "Did Lindsay give you the shorts?"

I nod.

She flicks cigarette ash into the water. "And what would your parents think?"

I cross my legs, tucking my feet underneath me. "You won't tell them, will you?"

"Of course not, not if you don't want me to. I think they look nice on you. Can you imagine your father's face if he saw?" Bubbie laughs.

"Should I...should I not wear them?"

"Oh, Ellie, wear whatever the hell you want. Your parents feel all funny about legs, and now even I'm acting crazy."

Sighing, I lean back in the chair and let my arms dangle over the armrests. "There's no men here to see me, no people really, so I don't think it really matters. I won't wear them when we go into Northbrook or anything."

"I'm sorry, I shouldn't have said anything."

"No, I don't care."

"You know, I haven't seen your mother's legs since nineteen seventy."

I glance at Bubbie. "Seventeen years ago?"

"Yep," she says. We both start giggling.

"I don't even know what they look like," I say.

"Oh, they're very nice. Your mother was athletic once. She has good calf muscles from skiing."

"I can't imagine Ima on skis."

"She just flew along. Didn't like moguls. She liked the feeling of flying. I guess she flies in a different way now." Bubbie shrugs.

"I'd like to fly like that, over snow and down hills."

"I've never taken you or Neshama away because of *Shabbos*."

I nod.

The sun slides behind the island and mosquitoes start buzzing around my head.

"What day is it?" I ask.

Bubbie closes one eye. "Saturday, I think."

"We missed *Shabbos*!" I sit upright, grip the arms of the chair.

Bubbie stretches her arms over her head, yawns. "I guess we did. I feel well rested, don't you?"

"Bubbie, we didn't light candles!"

"We could do them now."

"It's a day late."

"Oh, c'mon, just pretend."

I shake my head. "It's not the same."

I wander up to the cottage. If I were at home we'd be doing *Havdalah*, the prayers for the end of *Shabbos*. Ima and Abba are probably celebrating in Jerusalem. I scuff my sandal on the wood floor and sink into one of the orange recliners and rotate back and forth until I'm sleepy.

THE NEXT MORNING after prayers, breakfast and swimming, I settle in the hammock. A light breeze blows across the bay. I prop my ocean encyclopedia on my chest and let my eyes close. When Lindsay leaned toward me licking the glass, I saw the deep cleft between her breasts. I imagine my hand reaching out to her shoulder, stroking her collarbone, moving over her skin. A delicious tingle runs through me. My eyes fly open. What the *hell* am I thinking?

I flip to a picture of a narwhal.

Boys, Ellie, you're supposed to like boys. Right. Like… I don't know any boys. They go to a different school, sit in a different part of the synagogue, look away when we walk by. There's that guy at the supermarket Neshama thinks is cute. He has nice eyes, and his hair is the same strawberry blond as Lindsay's, except hers is long and rippled and soft, and oh, the ripples fall over her breasts.

Omigod. I lie stunned, my heart thumping. I flap my hands and pull at my hair. I'm thinking about a girl, and she's not even Jewish.

I can't be. I'm class monitor. I go to science fair. I'm the kind of girl who doesn't even think about boys.

Who never thinks about boys.

I won't be in love with her, I just won't. I'll just stop right now. There, done.

I get out of the hammock and march up the gravel road into the trees. I just want to be like her. That's right—the breasts, the hair and the way she talks, confident like Neshama, snappy like Bubbie, able to leap from canoes and gyrate in bikinis. I lean against an ash tree, dizzy. Omigod, *has va'halila*, please, not this. I just want to be normal.

Please, please, please.

Everyone I know is a pair—male and female. Adam and Eve, Avram and Sarah, Isaac and Rebecca, Jacob and Leah and Rachel. Okay, they're a threesome, but Isaac is key. Romeo and Juliet, Bo and Hope.

This isn't the first time I've thought about a girl this way. Last year I was obsessed with Hadassah Sternberger, our school council president. I admired the confident way she organized the mitzvah committee, the way she could stand up and talk in front of the whole school. At night I dreamed about touching her pale white skin and her pretty black hair, or what she looked like underneath her school uniform. I'd wake with a jolt from these dreams, sweaty and disoriented, and then spend the next couple of days blushing like crazy whenever I passed her in the hall. I was relieved when she graduated last spring.

There's supposed to be some nice David or Isaac in my future, medium height, maybe even muscled and tall as well as hairy. Yes, I'll be Ellie Cohen, or Ellie Rabinowitz, wife of some Jacob or Daniel. I close my eyes and try to imagine myself next to him. Holding hands, okay; kissing, not bad. But not like Lindsay. I sit on the ground and lean against the tree.

I can just see it. I'll be walking down the aisle in Ima's wedding dress with the lace sleeves. Abba and Ima look so proud. Neshama is my beautiful bridesmaid, and there'll be Lindsay smiling at me under the *chuppah*, the wedding canopy, wearing jean shorts and a white bikini top, her veil flowing. I'm heading toward her, propelled by this crazy swelling in my heart, this feeling I might burst. My legs are like jelly, and I'm almost at the end of the aisle. I'm so close I can almost hold her hand. Just a few more minutes, and I'll get to kiss her. Suddenly I see Ima, Abba and Neshama staring at me.

Ima gasps and falls into hysterics.

Neshama shrieks, "That's *so* disgusting, Ellie. You want to do IT with a girl?"

"A *shonda*," Abba booms, "my Ellie with a *shiksa*!" He spits. "Feh, feh, feh."

Only Bubbie is happy. "Serves your crazy parents right." She laughs, her mouth getting bigger and bigger until it turns into a black hole swallowing up the guests. Even Lindsay disappears into the vortex.

When I try to go home, Neshama stops me. "Don't you know? They're sitting *shivah* for you. Do you know how much baking I had to do for *your* mourners?"

Lightning will leap down from the heavens, rivers will flood, tornadoes will spin. There will be locusts, hail and fire. First born children will suddenly perish, which means Abba, Ima and Neshama will all die slow and agonizing deaths.

"No!" I leap up. Then I drop down to the ground, nervous energy ratcheting through me, and manage five measly push-ups before I collapse, panting.

I find Bubbie down on the dock. "Mini-golf, let's play mini-golf."

She looks up from her book. "Now? Isn't Lindsay coming over soon?"

"Yes, let's go now."

"Do you want to see if Lindsay wants to come?"

"No! I mean, let's just go."

"Did you two have a fight or something?"

"No, I just thought we could do something, the two of us. Mini-golf and ice cream."

"Okay, okay, let me just get changed."

I get Bubbie's keys and hat for her while she puts on shorts and a T-shirt and freshens her lipstick.

"Hurry."

"What's with you? It's not going to close or disappear."

I only relax once we pull onto the highway.

Mini-golf turns out to be even stupider than I expected, a little ball in a little hole, with silly obstacles. An ornamental plastic farmer and his wife swing over the final hole. One more happy pair.

Lindsay comes over in the evening. I'm sitting on the dock with my prayer book, trying to do the evening prayers I haven't done since I got to the cottage.

"Where were you this afternoon?"

"Mini-golf."

"I thought you hated ball sports."

"I do. Mini-golf isn't a sport."

"Well, do you want to go for a paddle now?"

I glance over at her freckled shoulder, her deep bluish green eyes. Say no. Say you don't feel well. "Um, sure."

I go up to the cottage to get my life jacket. Stupid, stupid, stupid.

When I come back down, Lindsay is standing on the dock, the fading sun lighting up her hair like fire. Run away, just run away and leave. I slowly make my way toward her, but instead of getting in the canoe I dive into the lake, the cool water stopping the sick feeling charging through me.

Three

For the next two weeks I spend the mornings alone. I never go over to Lindsay's. Instead I wait until she comes over, which is usually every afternoon. We paddle around the bay and into the marsh, or swim off one of our docks. If it rains, we play Monopoly or gin rummy with Bubbie. The mornings get cooler, and the adult loons have left their babies behind.

Today, Lindsay calls to ask me to go canoeing. After our paddle, we lie on her dock in our swimsuits. The sun scorches my skin. "How long are you staying?" I ask.

"We're supposed to leave next week. You?"

"The week after next."

Only one more week to try and walk like Lindsay, match her snappy answers. Only one more week to stare at her breasts when I think she isn't looking. And an eternity to hate myself for doing it.

Lindsay rolls over and her hair tickles my shoulder. I brush the hair away from my shoulder. I pause, my hand hesitating. Just one curl, and then I'll stop. Don't, Ellie, don't.

I reach out and finger the wet blond end. She doesn't notice.

"Want me to brush your hair?" I ask.

"It'll frizz," she says, her voice sleepy.

"You can jump in the water again."

Lindsay yawns, then nods. "Just don't pull too hard." She sits up and slips on sunglasses. I comb the tangles out from the ends of her spun taffy hair. She leans back against my upright knees, her skin warm on mine. When I get the knots out, I draw the brush over her head, rippled hair spilling over my legs. Lindsay drops her head all the way back, mouth relaxed, hands loose by her sides. She breathes long and slow, eyes closed.

I rub a long curl against my cheek. Heat runs from my toes up my legs. Then slowly, I comb my fingers over her scalp, down over her shoulders.

Lindsay shivers and lets out a small "Ahhh."

I pause a moment, hesitating. I trail my hand lightly down her arm.

Lindsay jerks away. "*What* are you doing?"

I'm still holding her hair. "I just thought…" The heat in my legs lodges in my stomach.

We stare at each other for a long moment. I clench my hands, my heart thumping.

"I think I'll go up for lunch." She stands up.

"Oh," I whisper.

She grabs her beach towel and T-shirt and backs away from me.

I exhale a breath I didn't know I was holding, my arms limp in my lap. Leaning back on the dock, I close my eyes. Her scalp was warm in my hands.

She liked it, I know she did.

Lindsay calls from the porch, "Do you want some lunch?"

I look up and shade my eyes. I can't imagine what I'll eat there, but I don't want to go home either. I slowly make my way up to the cottage, sun-dazed and humming with the feel of Lindsay's hair.

The kitchen in Lindsay's cottage is entirely white— the appliances, the counters and the cabinets.

We are quiet, not really looking at each other. "Are you sure you don't want a sandwich?" Lindsay asks. She rummages in the refrigerator.

"Nah, I don't think so." Lindsay has ham and cheese out.

"Lemonade?"

"Sure." I sit on a stool on the opposite side of the counter from Lindsay. I can't help watching the curve of her bum in her black bathing suit as she pours juice into a plastic glass. Her hair hangs loose down her back.

The phone rings, making both of us jump. Lindsay picks up.

"Hello? Oh, hi." She slumps over her plate. "Okay, I guess. Fine...yeah...nothing..." She studies her hair for split ends, leaning against the counter. "No, Craig's not here... No, no one. It's totally boring...Yeah, yeah...talk to you later...No, she doesn't want to...bye."

"Was that a friend?"

"Richard." Lindsay peels an onion.

"Who?"

"My father." She doesn't look up.

"Oh, does he ever come up here?"

"No, he's a dick." Lindsay slices the onion, her lips pressed together.

"Why's he a dick?"

"He just is." Lindsay pulls a jar of mustard out of the refrigerator.

"Do you ever see him?"

"Do you ever stop asking questions?" Lindsay puts down the mustard.

"Just curious." My hands twist behind my back. "So, do you?"

Lindsay glares at me, then she sighs. "You really want to know? He shows up for my birthday, takes Maureen—that's my mom—and me somewhere expensive for dinner and we all pretend to like each other. He gives me cool presents"—she holds out her leg to show off a gold ankle bracelet below her muscled calf—"and Maureen and Richard try not to bag on each other's current lovers. Any more questions?"

"Lovers?" The word pops out of my mouth.

"Yeah." Lindsay leers. "Looo-vers." She leans toward me over the counter, her breasts pressing against her bathing suit. She snickers and taps her fingers on the counter. "Why is that so embarrassing to you?" She slowly licks the mustard off the tip of the knife. I blush even more.

Lindsay's mom pops out of a bedroom and joins us in the kitchen. "Hi, it's Ellie, right?" She daubs sunscreen on her tanned shoulders.

Lindsay steps away from me and spreads mustard on slices of white bread.

"Yes, hi." I slip off the stool and take a few steps toward the long oak kitchen table, out of the way.

"Maureen, we're out of milk again." Lindsay dumps the empty carton in the trash.

"Put it on the list." Lindsay's mom wears hot pink shorts, her large breasts hoisted, flattened and pushed together under a black running bra. Her streaked blond ponytail pokes over her sun visor. "I can't wait for you to start driving."

"I'm not gonna be your servant," Lindsay mumbles, scribbling a list on a pad of paper. "We're also out of ginger ale, marshmallows and Swiss."

"Gin too." Lindsay's mom bends to tie her shoe.

Lindsay peers over the counter. "*More* gin?"

"Lindsay." Her mother's tone hardens into a warning.

"What?" Lindsay's slanted eyes open wide.

Maureen straightens up and frowns at her. "What are you girls going to do this afternoon?"

"Well." Lindsay leans on the counter. "I thought we'd start with vodka shots, move on to mixed drinks, down on the dock of course."

"That's not funny."

"Why not, Mother?"

I step farther back into the living room, pretending to read the newspaper on the green couch.

Lindsay's mom stands staring at her, legs spread, hands on hips. Lindsay takes a bite of her sandwich, staring back. A moment passes, and I sink lower on the couch.

Dave, Maureen's boyfriend, pulls open the sliding door. "Are you ready?" He wears a baseball cap and tank top, chest hair curling over the neckline.

He puts his arm around her shoulder, his lips close to her ear. "Are you ready?" he repeats.

Lindsay rolls her eyes and turns away.

Maureen nods and lets Dave guide her out.

"You shouldn't let her get to you," he says from the porch.

"You shouldn't let her get to you," Lindsay mimics. She drinks directly from a two-liter bottle of cola, shoving the refrigerator closed with her hip.

Lindsay stomps around the kitchen, opening and closing drawers, picking at her sandwich and a bag of salt-and-vinegar chips. She disappears into a bedroom and comes out wearing sunglasses, a pair of jean shorts over her bathing suit, her feet slipped into green flip-flops. "I'm going to get some ice cream at the campground. Are you coming?"

We head up the shaded gravel road through the trees to the highway. Dry heat breaks over us, the asphalt magnifying the sun's glare. The buzz of blackflies and the hum of hydro wires fills the air with a constant electric drone, like heat making noise. Only the roar of passing cars breaks the monotony. Beyond the ribbon of gravel at the shoulder, black-eyed Susans and Queen Anne's Lace bloom. The road stretches ahead of us, a shimmering black curve.

Lindsay walks ahead, her hands clenched at her sides, her flip-flops sucking at her heels. A snake flits out of the ditch, surprising me. I crouch at the side of the road to watch it blend in green and brown among the scrub.

"Did you see the snake?" I call to her.

Lindsay whirls around. "Why would I care?"

Lindsay doesn't say anything until she has an ice-cream cone and a small, brown paper bag full of jelly worms, gummy bears and jujubes. We sit at a picnic table under the shade of some elm trees by the water. Off to the side is a grassy area leading to the beach and a boat launch smelling of gasoline. I pull down my baseball cap to shade my eyes from the noon sun and suck on a Popsicle.

The water laps blue and gold from the sun's rays against the weathered boards of the boat dock, weeds gently moving back and forth in the water. Out in the bay beyond the point, seagulls circle the few lone white pines on Horseshoe Island. They dip around the tall branches, screeching and garbling, finally come to rest in the placid waters. The sky stretches blue, thin white clouds slowly drifting.

"Jujube?" Lindsay offers the bag to me.

I shake my head.

"Your parents still together?" Lindsay asks.

I nod.

"Money?"

"Pardon?"

"Are your parents together for financial reasons or because they just can't be bothered to split up?"

My parents would never hold hands in public, or even in front of me, yet I see the way they listen to each other. "I-I think they like each other."

"Really?" Lindsay looks me right in the eye, looks at me so hard I twist in my seat.

"Yeah," I respond. "They went to Israel together for the summer."

Lindsay whistles and shakes her head.

"Can I ask you a question?"

Lindsay pushes her sunglasses down her nose and narrows her eyes at me, her lip curling. "Only one?"

I ignore the teasing slant of her eyes. "Why do you call your mother Maureen?"

Lindsay stops smiling and looks out at the kids playing in the sandpit. She turns back to me. "'Cause then she listens."

WHEN I GET back to the cottage, I join Bubbie for lunch.

"Can I ask you something?"

"Sure."

"Did you ever do anything really bad? I mean when you were a kid."

"No, but your mom did."

"Really?" I put down my tomato sandwich.

Bubbie laughs. "I'm just kidding. Your mother never did anything. Why do you ask?"

"Oh, well, no reason."

Bubbie looks at me over her glass. "What, did you eat pork? Did you forget *Shabbos* again? Did you have gelatin?"

"Forget it."

"Aw, I'm sorry. I'll stop. Let's see. I think I stole a magazine from a store and, well, of course I was never home on time, and I smoked. Nothing I think I'll go to hell for."

I sigh and down the rest of my lemonade.

LINDSAY DOESN'T COME over the next day, so I wander over to her place in the evening. She is sitting at the top of the porch stairs, her hair scraped into two tight braids.

"Hey," she says.

I sit tentatively next to her. "I brought my star chart," I say, pulling out a paperback book.

"Wha—?"

"My star chart. I'm going to find the Little Dipper and maybe some—"

Lindsay bursts out laughing.

"What?"

"You are *such* a geek."

I shrug and flip open the book. As long as she's laughing. "I can never find Cassiopeia." I lean back on my elbows, gaze up at the sky.

Lindsay wraps her arms around her legs, taps her feet on the wooden deck. "Stars are boring. How about Truth or Dare?"

"Oh, I'm really bad at that." A slice of moon sinks through the clear night sky behind the trees on the island.

"Truth or dare?" Lindsay repeats.

"Truth," I say, still looking at the sky. "I think that's the Little Dipper."

"Okay, truth. Ever kissed a boy?"

"Did you know the moon controls the tides?"

"Ellie."

I sit up. "No, but I've practiced for it."

Lindsay glances over. "Pillows?"

"No, on my sister." I check the star map and squint back up at the sky, avoiding Lindsay's look. "If that's the Little Dipper then…"

Lindsay's eyes open wide. "You're kidding, right?"

I shake my head.

"Ew. I always used my pillow or arm."

"It's not the same." When we were little, my sister and I used to practice kissing with our mouths clamped tight.

Lindsay pauses, impressed, looking at me, head cocked to the side. "Okay, you dare me something."

I'd like to dare her to kiss me, to let me touch her long strawberry-blond hair. I stare out over the lake shimmering in the moonlight.

"You're so slow!" Lindsay stands up. I cringe and tense my shoulders. "Okay, I'll choose truth instead, and I'll answer the question I gave you. Yes, I've kissed a boy. There. Now, how about a dare—"

"Wait, what was it like?"

"The kiss? Wet."

"Did you…did you use your tongue?"

"Of course."

"So, is he your boyfriend now?"

"Nah."

"Why not?"

"I didn't like him that much."

"You still kissed him?"

Lindsay tosses her head. "Enough questions. Truth or dare?"

"Dare."

"Okay, I double-dog dare you to skinny-dip to the raft and back." She leans over me, hands on her hips.

I look up. "Skinny-dip?"

Lindsay flicks a braid over her shoulder. She nods.

I pause, imagining the cool water on my skin. "Will you come?"

"You mean you dare me back?"

I shiver and nod. A breeze stirs the trees. Strands of her hair brush against my shoulder. I clutch the star chart to my chest, my stomach forming a sharp fist, like fingernails pressing into me.

"Last one in is a rotten egg," she says.

We sprint across the lawn, pulling off our T-shirts and bras, laughing as we run through the dark. I stop at the end of the grass to wriggle out of my shorts and underwear, getting a quick glimpse of Lindsay's breasts. The night extends black like velvet, the stars glimmering like sequins, the moon casting pools over the lake. I run straight across the dock, my legs still churning as I hit the water. A delicious cold shock breaks the nervous energy circulating through me. Just as I surface, Lindsay dives, ever graceful, her naked body white in the night. She swims a furious smooth line past me toward the raft. I do my best front crawl behind her, my arms choppy, legs splashing.

When we grasp the ladder, I can feel Lindsay's warmth beside me, hear the rapidness of her breath, see the tops of her breasts. Our legs brush each other as we tread water. My nipples harden into tight buds in the cold water.

"Ellie?"

"Yeah?"

"It's your turn."

"I dared you back."

She flicks water in my face. "Doesn't count."

"Ah." I pause. "I...I can't think of anything."

Lindsay spits a mouthful of water at me. "You're pathetic."

"Dare me something instead," I beg.

Lindsay pauses, moves closer to me. "Hmm..." She furrows her brow. Then she leans over to my ear. My teeth start to chatter, goose bumps forming up my arms.

"I dare you," she whispers, her breath warm, "to disappear."

"What?" I jerk away. My face falls. I don't want to leave. I want to stay by her warm body in the lake, the two of us in the moonlight.

"You know, leave and not come back." Lindsay smiles.

"Where would I go?"

"I don't know, just away."

I push hair out of my face. "That's the stupidest thing ever. It'd take hours to just walk to Cloyne."

"Who said walk?" Lindsay calmly treads water.

"You mean hitch? Isn't that dangerous?"

"I've done it before. Do you dare me back?"

"No."

"Dare me back."

"Forget it."

"C'mon."

"No! I wanna dare you something else," I blurt out.

The screen door slams up at the cottage, and we hear Lindsay's mom on the porch.

"I want—," I whisper.

"I'm cold," Lindsay interrupts. "Race you back." She plunges down into the water, leaving me hanging on the raft. The moon sinks behind the island, and the porch lights flick off.

I let go, water closing over my head. My hair swims around me in a brown cloud.

I creep out of the water and dress, shivering, behind a tree. Lindsay is waiting for me with a flashlight from the cottage. Her hair leaves a long wet patch down her back. She walks me back through the trees, waving her flashlight across the path. When she bends down to tie her shoe, I slip into the trees. After a moment of rustling branches, I'm motionless behind a birch. I press my back against the peeling bark.

"Ellie?" Lindsay shines the light into the trees near me. I dart back, crouching in the grass.

"Ellie?"

"I'm right here."

She whirls around, shining the light in my eyes. "*What are you doing?*"

"Disappearing."

Her lip curls into a sneer.

"And re-appearing," I add. "You dared me."

Lindsay scowls. "You don't get it, do you?"

"Get what?"

She turns on her heel and runs back to her cottage, a haze of mosquitoes following her.

When I stumble out of the trees, most of the cottage lights are already out. Bubbie has gone to bed, her radio playing fifties' music. I wander about, skim a layer of dust off a pine end table, drag my fingers around the brass lamp and the pictures frames. In the bedroom, I slip off my Star of David necklace and put it in my bag with my skirts.

I OVERSLEEP THE next morning. When I awake, I am sweat-streaked and disoriented. My stomach feels queasy, and a nervous energy tingles in my feet. I stomp them on the bare wood floor.

Gray clouds blanket the horizon. The air is heavy, moisture hanging like a layer of city smog. Bubbie is out on the dock. "Summertime, and the living is easy," she bellows, her voice rough. I wave to her and head back into the woods with my prayer book. Perspiration forms under my arms and along my hairline. I step off the path between the sparse branches of two fir trees, brushing away loose branches and twigs until I have a small clearing. My morning prayers fall automatically, without thought, off my tongue. I chant under my breath, "*Modah Ani Lefanecha, Melech Chai Vekayam.*" I am grateful to you, living and enduring King. When I finish, the humidity still wraps thickly around me, through me.

I add a few extra English prayers of my own. *Please stop me from doing anything bad.* I crouch down in the pine needles, pick up a dry birch branch and balance it against another bough, creating an arch as high as my waist. I step back to eye the curve of wood between the firs, and add more branches, forming a small dome. Inside my tree hut I sit cross-legged and try to recite psalms. I sigh and drop my head forward. Lindsay's skin shimmered warm and wet and close.

Back down at the shore, I watch a frog tremble in the weeds, its cheeks quivering. I bend down in the mud, cup my hands, and reach out and snap my palms around the frog. It's smooth, not slimy the way I expected. The tiny feet tickle, and I let it go.

Lindsay stands on the end of her dock, skipping stones over the calm gray lake. The rocks make small plinking noises across the still water. When I join her, she slumps in a wooden deck chair and scratches a trio of mosquito bites up her arm.

I sit next to her and pull my knees into my chest under my baggy T-shirt. Two loons swim out by the island, diving down and resurfacing.

"I built this hut, this tree hut."

"A tree hut?"

"Yeah, wanna see it?"

Lindsay turns and watches the loons take off and fly over the trees. "No, not really."

The screen door slides open and we turn to see Dave coming down the stairs with a beer and the newspaper. "Crap," she says, "he's coming this way." We wave at Dave and head to the path through the trees. "Okay," she says, "what did you want to show me?"

I lead her up behind the cottage, halfway up the road to the highway and along the old overgrown path. She eyes me suspiciously when I lift a branch for her to go into the hut. We balance on our toes in the small dark space under the branches. Our knees bump, and I bury my hands in the dry pine needles to balance myself. A cool breeze lifts some of the humidity.

"It's quiet here," Lindsay says.

I nod, squinting in the dim light. My legs start to cramp. "It's better if you sit, I think." We shift our feet in the small space, trying to put our butts down without disturbing the branches. Lindsay is first to lose her balance. She grabs my hand, sending small currents down my spine. Her other hand grazes my thigh. We fall over, holding tight to each other, sticks tumbling down on us. I want to laugh and cry, but I'm breathing too hard. I'm holding Lindsay and she's laughing, a quick layer of sweat forming between the skin of our legs.

"I'm sorry, Ellie," she says, her mouth open with laughter. "Oh, Ellie," she says, "I'm sorry." She can't stop laughing.

We stumble out of the trees into a clearing surrounded by sumac bushes, the grass flat like a cushion from where deer have lain. Lindsay flops down on her back, still giggling. I pick a milkweed pod and lie down next to her.

"Look." I break open the green shell to show her the layers of white feather-like plant inside. "It's like a female peacock."

Lindsay touches the pod, sap dripping.

"Monarch butterflies feed on them."

"Uh-huh." Lindsay rolls over on her side. "Last night in the water..."

My shoulders tense, a film of sweat covering my back. "Yeah?"

"I know what you wanted to dare me."

I freeze, my chest tightening. I stare at her. She doesn't have her usual teasing look, the manipulative gleam in her eyes. She touches my bare arm, milkweed sticky on my skin. Raising herself on one elbow, she hesitates, moves her lips close to my ear. "I dare you to kiss me," she whispers. "I want to know what it's like—to kiss a girl."

The earth seems to tilt, my pulse races. I roll over on my side and stare at her. She presses her mouth against mine, her lips stiff at first and then soft and warm. My arm slides tentatively over her waist, down the curve of her hip. Lindsay holds her breath, her eyes closed. She doesn't stop me.

THE NEXT MORNING I wake up early, shivering under a thin blanket, dawn barely etching the gray sky. Bubbie and I drink tea, bundled in sweaters on the porch, and watch the baby loons. She passes me the binoculars. I can't focus. I drum my fingers on the edge of my chair, keep checking my watch.

When it is finally late enough, so I won't seem too eager, I run to Lindsay's. My feet are light and quick through the trees, past the leaning birch, over the spruce log, past the marsh with the rusting car. I force myself to slow down at the sumac trees at the edge of Lindsay's lawn. I stop at the porch stairs. The blinds are drawn, the doors shut, the patio furniture put away. My heart thumps. Down on the water a whippoorwill calls *weeee-heeee*. I walk around to the front of the cottage. Lindsay's mom's Jeep is gone. Maybe they just went for groceries or mini-golf. Peering in the front door of the cottage, I see the magazines are neatly stacked, the fans still, the counters clean.

I pace up and down the porch. Then I kick a pile of pinecones onto the grass. Shivering in my fleece, I lean against the railing Lindsay's mom didn't want. I didn't even get to ask her if we could meet back in the city.

THE SUN BEATS down hot on my back, the water cool around me. My right arm comes up over my head, slips into the water. Cup and pull. Then my left arm—inhale—splashing into the water. I swim a few more strokes, shoulders contracting before reaching for the air mattress. I spit out a mouthful of water.

"You're doing great," Bubbie tells me. She lies on the mattress, paddling beside me.

I nod, out of breath. It's not quite the way I wanted to swim to the island. However, as Bubbie says, it's better than becoming fish food.

I rest my head on the hot plastic, close my eyes against the bright sun, kick my legs. I glance over at Lindsay's empty dock: the lawn furniture and fishing gear are gone, even the canoe is put away in the shed.

Bubbie follows my gaze. "I haven't seen Lindsay in a few days."

"She's gone."

"Pardon?"

"Home. They went home."

"Oh, I guess it's that time of year. We'll have to pack up after lunch if we want to be in time to get your parents from the airport."

"She didn't say good-bye."

Bubbie frowns. "Maybe something came up."

I shake my head.

Bubbie shades her eyes, looks at me. "She's a slippery one."

I nod, avoiding Bubbie's glance, and slide off the mattress. I push myself under water for as long as I can before breaking into a front crawl. Bubbie follows along beside me on the air mattress.

I rest again, this time halfway across the bay. Our dock seems far away, the logs on the other side equally hazy.

"I caught a frog the other day," I tell Bubbie.

"Tell me about frogs."

"*Phylum chordata, class lissamphibia*—that means it's got smooth skin," I tell her. "I always thought frogs would feel slimy. They're smooth, just like their name."

"Do you know those things from school?"

I laugh. "Bubbie, religious girls don't need to know about frogs or birds or fish, except to know if they are kosher."

Our days in school are divided into religious studies in the morning and everything else in the afternoon. Science is crammed into two hours one afternoon a week. We read the chapter in our textbooks, answer the questions. The ecology sections are in the back of the book, and we never get there by the end of the year. Once I asked my teacher how dinosaur bones could be older than creation. The teacher said God put the bones there to test our faith.

"Are frogs kosher?" Bubbie asks.

"Nope. No fins or gills."

"Oh, they taste like chicken."

"So I'm not missing anything then?"

"You'd like to study more about frogs, about nature, wouldn't you?"

I laugh. "Yeah, sure."

Bubbie just nods, and so I swim again, practicing my breaststroke, like a frog. Bubbie follows on the mattress.

When we reach the island we stand on a fallen log, holding onto the mattress. "Looks a lot like the other side," I tell Bubbie.

"Yep." She points to a blue heron skimming across the water. I rest in the shade a few minutes. Bubbie says, "We'd better get going."

"Five more minutes?"

"You don't want to be late for your parents."

I sigh and take one more look around. I grab hold of the air mattress next to Bubbie and together we push it with long lazy kicks.

AT THE END of the day I stand on the dock, gazing out at the island. The sun sets pink and gold over the bay. I stay one more minute and then wrap my arms around a tree trunk before leaving to join Bubbie in the car. Now I know the feel of wet pine needles on my arm, the crunch of dry leaves in my palm, small berries rolling under my feet.

In the city I know all the surfaces already: concrete, linoleum, plastic, Formica, porcelain, all cold and hard. Polished wood at best, but with a layer of paint over top.

Four

Ima bursts out of the airport, her eyes glittering with an alarming intensity. Abba follows her, luggage-laden, jetlag etching his smile. They climb into the car, showering us with kisses.

"You had a good time?" Bubbie asks.

"Wonderful," Ima says. She leans forward and squeezes my hand before putting on her seatbelt.

"Absolutely amazing," Abba says.

Bubbie pulls out of the airport into the maze of sunscorched highway.

"It was just incredible," Abba sighs. "When we got off the plane we could smell orange blossoms. And I tell you, the land feels different there."

Bubbie rolls her eyes.

At the house, Abba opens windows, turns on taps, sifts mail into piles. Ima grabs my hand and pulls me up the stairs with her suitcase. "I have so much to tell you." She closes the bedroom door and turns on the air conditioner. When she pulls off her blue cotton scarf, her rich brown hair cascades over her shoulders, sweaty and threaded with gray.

I notice the leather dye of her new sandals has bled into her white socks.

Most of Ima and Abba's room is taken up by the bed with its patchwork comforter. A low wooden dresser is jammed below the window with framed pictures of Abba's parents, Bubba Rosa and Zeyda Yuri, on it. The air conditioning gradually cools the room, cutting the thick humidity. I sit on the bed and stretch my T-shirt over my knees.

"So? Tell me about the trip."

Ima kneels on the floor beside her suitcase and starts filling a laundry basket with crumpled blouses and balled-up socks. "It was unbelievable," she says. Outside a dog barks. "Wonderful," she repeats.

"Did you see the sea?"

"The sea? We went to Israel. It's a desert."

"Sand dunes?" I imagine sand fanning out, licked by the wind's tongue into crescent-shaped grooves.

"No, it's more rocky and hilly."

"Oh."

"But it's ours." Ima's eyes flicker with excitement. She leans back on her heels, her arms wrapped around her legs.

I nod, letting my hair fall forward to hide my face. Neshama and I have had long discussions about whose land it is.

"That slice of sand and desert with its heat and all its troubles, it's ours," Ima continues. "Here is all kinds of different people, not Jews." She takes a deep breath. "There the land is ours."

"The *Kotel*, did you go to the *Kotel*?" For weeks before Ima left, all she spoke about was the Western Wall.

"Oh." She flushes. "I'll have to tell you about that later, when Neshama comes."

I stare at her sparkling eyes.

"Here," she says, digging in her bag, "I brought you something, a present." She pulls out a small plastic bag. I expect a book or a necklace, something Jewish.

"For you," she says stroking the bag, "I have brought"—her voice dropping to a whisper—"a perfect Israeli specimen."

She sits down on the bed bedside me and pulls out a fruit, round like a tomato, the color of an orange. I roll the rubbery sphere, my brow furrowed. It smells of the earth, not tangy or citric. "You snuck fruit through customs?"

Ima ignores my raised eyebrows. "What tastes like a peach, looks like a tomato, but is the color of an orange?"

"You brought me a riddle?" I squint at Ima.

She smiles again and pulls my head close to hers until I can smell her familiar lavender scent. "Sultan's peach, Roman tomato, King David's orange," she whispers. She picks the fruit out of my palm. "This persimmon is my Israel."

She pulls a pocketknife out of her suitcase and slices the fruit into quarters. I pull the skin off with my teeth. The smooth peach-like flesh tastes like perfume.

"This persimmon is like smashing the cup at the end of a wedding," she says.

"What?"

"It reminds me of our tenuous hold on Jerusalem. We own the land now, but around every corner I saw shades of the past, shades of how light our hold on the country is.

Sure, we build new settlements to…to sink our teeth into the soil, but it's only sand. It crumbles, gives way. In this fruit"— she grasps the persimmon's remaining brown seeds, her knuckles white—"I see every army that ever passed through Jerusalem, and I understand how lucky we are to have it."

"Uh…yeah."

Ima cradles her bag of persimmons in her lap before putting them on the bedside table next to the small copper lamp. "Did you have a good time with Bubbie?"

"Yeah, I had a great summer. I swam a lot and learned to paddle a canoe." Heat crawls up my face. "So you didn't swim in the Mediterranean?"

Ima zips up the empty suitcase and shakes her head.

Of course they didn't, not my modest, white-skinned parents. Not on the beach in Tel Aviv where I've seen pictures of scantily-clad Israelis in bikinis with uncovered hair, naked limbs. Like Lindsay. I start to blush again and duck my head so Ima can't see. If I ever get to Israel, the ocean will be the first place I visit.

Ima has had a summer of sand and dust, while I have been learning to swim. Crouching by the water's edge, I looked at crayfish, rising early to push a canoe through the quiet water to chase loons around the bay. I think of the wet mulch at the edge of Lake Missisagagon, the mist rising off the water.

"Oh, here, I brought you something else. It's from the desert and also the sea." Ima rifles through her straw shoulder bag, pulling out a handful of mints and a film canister.

"Hold out your hands." She pries off the lid of the canister and pours gritty bits of sand and some tiny white shells into my hands. "It's from Mitzpe Ramon, this crater in the south."

I stare at the shells. "By the sea?"

"No, in the middle of the desert."

"There are shells there?"

"Yes, I thought you'd like that." Ima smiles at me.

I sift the sand, poke at the gritty bits, the small white swirls. I imagine the sea raging across the sand, then departing, leaving remnants on the shores. I squeeze the bits in my palms. "What is this, evidence of Noah?"

Ima's back to sorting laundry. "Maybe." She glances up at me. "Where's your necklace?"

My hands fly to my neck. "I took it off to swim."

"It was Bubba Rosa's."

"I know. I just forgot to put it back on." I go get it from the suitcase under my bed and fasten the chain around my neck. I lower the neckline of my T-shirt to show Ima the small gold heart with the Star of David carved on it. The necklace feels tight around my neck.

"Beautiful," she says and kisses my forehead.

THE CAMP BUS drops Neshama at home in the evening. She is tanned, blonder than before—streaks, I suspect—and carries one more bag than she left with. I peer at it suspiciously.

Ima hugs her. "How was camp?"

"Wonderful, amazing," she says.

Abba studies her outfit—a three-quarter-length-sleeve sundress with buttons down the front—before he kisses her.

Upstairs she nudges the imitation Louis Vuitton suitcase under her bed. I raise my eyebrows. She pushes me into the bathroom, pink pearl nails fluttering, while Ima goes to get a laundry basket.

"Contraband," she hisses.

I raise my eyebrows.

"Things for you too," she adds.

"From camp?"

She shoves me into the towel rack. "No, silly. We sneaked out." We hear Ima on the stairs. "Outlet mall," she whispers. "Wait till you see." She smiles and pulls her dress tight against her chest to show me the outline of her bra. It's not the shapeless beige kind Ima buys for us.

Neshama puts on a long-sleeve cardigan, covering her forearms. "Don't want to piss off Abba too soon."

"What's up?"

"Later," she hisses.

After my parents have gone to bed, the air conditioner droning in their room, Neshama pushes the lacy pillows and teddy bears off her bed and spreads out her new treasures on the pink bedspread. Neshama's room is stuffed. Her dresser is strewn with tubes of lipstick, nail polish and jars of makeup brushes. Fashion magazines and romance novels spill out from under her bed. A shelf holds her collection of music boxes.

I wedge my feet between the pillows and bears and watch her spread out short-sleeved V-neck T-shirts, and matching bra and underwear sets in stripes and lace trim. She pulls out a pair of slim-fit, faded Levis with orange tags and a button-up fly. "Here," she say. "These are for you."

I clasp the jeans to my face, breathe in their new cotton smell, feel the stiffness of the material. I have never had jeans before. "Thanks," I whisper. I get up and step into the pant legs, pull them up over my hips, struggling with the buttons. The jeans rest just below my belly button. I look in the mirror at the long smooth line of my legs.

"Check out your butt."

I peer over my shoulder and swivel my hips as if I'm in a TV commercial.

Neshama giggles. "One more present." She pushes a small pink plastic bag into my hands. I wrestle with the tissue and pull out a matching bra and panty set, satiny dark blue with only half cups and panties cut high on the sides. "It's the color I imagine the ocean might be."

I squeeze her tight.

"Perfect for your future honey."

I shoot her a sidelong glance.

"What?" she asks.

I sit down at her desk, shuffle her papers into piles. I kissed Lindsay in the clearing and her lips were warm and soft. "Not me, I mean, not now, I—"

"Just kidding." Neshama punches my shoulder. "Abba isn't really going to choose one of those pale, sick-looking *yeshiva buchers* for you."

"He'll find someone for you first."

"No, not me."

"Still leaving?"

"Yes." Neshama clasps a V-neck T-shirt. "Not much longer now." Her mouth forms a thin line. Cords stand out at her throat and temples.

"You still have another year of school, Ness." I fuss with the tissue paper, refolding the lingerie inside.

Neshama drops the T-shirt and sits on the edge of her bed, facing me. She stretches out her hands in front of her, her knuckles straining, nails glinting in the lamplight. She lets out a big breath. "I'm taking some math courses by correspondence. Then I can apply to university business programs for next fall."

My eyes open wide. "Have you told Ima and Abba yet?"

"They don't need to know. Not yet, anyway. Bubbie has already promised to help me with the tuition."

I tug at the edge of the sheet on Neshama's bed. My parents want us to become religious schoolteachers like them. "Oh," I say, too awed to add anything else.

We're silent a moment. Neshama pulls up her skirt and studies her shin.

"You never asked about the cottage," I say tentatively.

"How was the cottage?" She concentrates on picking an ingrown hair.

"It was good." I smile.

"Let me guess," Neshama says, still picking. "Bubbie snuck cigarettes, watched birds. You had cocktails at five, deli at six, and oh, you were all excited because you did something gross with amphibians. Right?"

"Yes, but there was more."

"Yeah, so?"

"There were other people there."

"Boys?" Neshama stops picking and looks up, suddenly interested.

I pause, not sure how to answer. "No, not boys. A girl. I made a friend. She's not Jewish."

"Big deal. Girls, shmirls. I had an entire summer— please—an entire life of girls."

I ponder this, the idea of a summer camp of nothing but girls. I turn to Neshama. "Look." I pull down the neckline of my blouse and show her the white strap marks of my bathing suit. "Bubbie bought me the suit."

Neshama looks at my shoulders. Then she opens her blouse at the neck. Her shoulders are perfectly golden without a single mark.

I sigh and get up to go. "Thanks for the contraband."

Back in my room, I tuck the clothes, along with Lindsay's jean cutoffs and tank top, into the suitcase under my bed.

NESHAMA HAS ALWAYS been waiting to escape. When we were little she was sure we were born into the wrong family and no one knew except us. According to her, we weren't supposed to be daughters of reborn Orthodox Jews, *ba'al t'shuva*, but part of a family of traveling circus performers or eclectic spiritual healers. At best she thought we belonged in Bubbie's "normal" world.

Neshama and I used to play a game we called Escape! "What if you need to leave fast?" Neshama would ask. "What would you take?" We'd each grab a bag or a suitcase, and we'd have a minute to pack. Then we'd meet in the basement to see what we'd taken. Sometimes the game was more elaborate. Neshama set the rules. "There's a fire in the house, or a knock at the door." Most of the time, we packed as if we wouldn't be coming back. Neshama always started with clothes and her small blue teddy bear—the bare essentials—and quickly moved to bigger heavier items, cramming her bags with felt pens and rainbow notepads, stuffed animals and her collection of *Little House on the Prairie* books.

I would spend most of the time deciding between a favorite book and three pairs of socks. When we met in the basement, Neshama struggled under the weight of her bag. I clutched a bar of soap, a toothbrush and a *siddur*.

"You'll be cold," she said.

"But clean," I replied. We stared at each other.

We stopped playing the game when Bubba Rosa, Abba's mother, died.

Abba's parents lived in a small apartment over their dry-cleaning and tailor shop off Yonge Street. I remember them as people who held fear in their backbones, in the angles of their shoulders, a tenseness Abba has inherited.

Abba's parents bent over the steamer, cut cloth, inhaled dry-cleaning chemicals and lived their whole lives within the confines of the shop. The front window allowed passersby a glimpse of Bubba Rosa eating a plate of cabbage salad or Zeyda sewing on his ancient Singer. Neshama once asked if he had brought the machine from Poland. Zeyda laughed. "I came with a pincushion, I should be so lucky." He always had a yellow pack of Chiclets for us in his breast pocket.

Zeyda once asked, "Who does Neshama look like?" He stroked her fine blond hair. Goldilocks, he called her.

"My sister," Bubba Rosa replied. "My sister who was."

WHEN BUBBA ROSA died, less than a year after Zeyda, Ima handed Neshama and me each a garbage bag when we went to clear out their apartment. They left behind broken china, cheap chachkas, endless pairs of pantyhose. I watched as their privacy was invaded. Ima cleared out drawers of faded saggy underwear, cabinets of medicines long out of date. As she packed shapeless dresses and worn shoes with broken laces, I heard Bubba Rosa's heavy accent, saw her old hands pressing a worn change purse full of silver dollars into my palms. I held a scarf Bubba had once woven through my hair with her old gnarled fingers, felt it thin and worn, heard it swish into the bag.

In the bedroom, Neshama and I found a suitcase under the bed. Inside were pairs and pairs of new underwear, socks, pantyhose all still in their cardboard packages. Bars of soap, a shaving kit, sweaters, cans of tuna and a bag of peanuts.

Neshama and I never mentioned the suitcase. We never played the packing game again.

Leaving was always Neshama's game, not mine. Now when I close my eyes, I see Lindsay beckoning to me as she glides by in her cherry-red canoe.

FRIDAY MORNING OF the Labor Day long weekend I wake to the churn of the washing machine, clothes flapping on the line, the dishwasher humming.

Time at the cottage was a blur. Here at home we mark the days, cutting the line sharp between regular and sacred time. We order our weeks, months, into neat segments: work and rest, holiday and ritual. We sit heavier in our chairs on Friday nights, let the wood take the weight of our spines.

"Two weeks until *yontif*," Abba says, rolling out dough for cookies he will freeze.

"Eight hours until *Shabbos*," Ima says, running the vacuum in the living room.

Eight hours. Enough time to move slowly in the humid heat, the windows open to birds and traffic. *Shabbos* doesn't start until sundown: seven forty. Time stretches out hot and slow.

I polish the *Shabbos* candles, set the table with wineglasses and the good china. When I'm finished, I fold laundry on the kitchen table: T-shirt sleeves in first, then bodies neatly tucked up. Underwear crotches up, sides in. I refold the tea towels Ima has shoved in the drawer.

Our kitchen is all yellow: both the sunshiny cupboards with their old metal handles and the lemony walls. The nicest thing about our kitchen is the hardwood floor, although it needs to be refinished. Everything else is awkward and old. The drawers either stick or come flying out, whisks, spatulas and soup ladles spilling to the floor. The tap drips or gushes, and the kitchen window sticks open or dangerously smashes down unless propped with a brick. The gold-flecked

Formica counters are knife-marked, rippled with age and crowded with porcelain containers: sugar, flour, coffee, tea. Abba couldn't bring himself to part with Bubba Rosa's old jars. The heavy meat grinder she used for making chopped liver takes up counter space beside the oven.

The window over the sink looks out on the narrow strip of our yard. Next to it, our yellowed fridge hums loudly. Neshama has clipped out pictures of new kitchens and taped them to the refrigerator, hoping Abba will take the obvious hint. He never does, although he did buy an extra freezer to hoard his baking.

Our rickety kitchen table sits between the pantry and the door to the hallway. Above the table is a black and white photo my Uncle Isaac took of Ima. In it she sits in our kitchen, her arms crossed over her pregnant belly. Her cheeks are full and flushed, a band of freckles across her nose making her look almost tanned and robust. Neshama stands on a chair, pigtails sprouting out the sides of her head, whispering to Ima, her small chubby hand cupped to her mouth.

"What was the secret?" Neshama always asks.

"I don't know," Ima says. "I only remember Bubba Rosa was over, teaching your father to bake."

Abba loves to bake. He forgets about his studies and teaching and spreads ingredients out on the counter: room-temperature eggs, butter, bags of flour, poppy seeds, squares of chocolate, tubs of sour cream. Then he mixes, stirs, kneads, licks and tastes. He listens to opera, his beard full of flour. "Raisins," he sings along with *Carmen* or *Aida*, and he dumps a handful of plump raisins into sweet cinnamon twists, or between layers of soft malleable dough. He makes *rugelach* with chocolate or cinnamon sugar filling, rich and oozing and buttery on your fingers. In his kitchen, blueberry Bundt cakes slide from pans, the slow suck of air hissing steam. He makes yeasty *challahs* with shiny yolk coating, flaky apple strudel dripping warm raisins and soft apple slices. His thin poppyseed cookies are delicious with tea. He makes *mandlebroit*, crumbling and nutty, for dunking in coffee. He bakes yeast rolls and sour-cream coffee cake and chocolate brownies, all of it producing rich aromas that waft through the kitchen and seep into the wallpaper on the stairs. Our kitchen is dingy and uneven, but saturated with the most delicious smells. "Your father bakes love," Ima says.

When I am done my chores, I wander up to my room and flop down on my bed. My room is similar in size to Neshama's, but without all the stuff. I have a blue quilt, a whale poster over my bed and gray shag carpet on the floor. Shells Bubbie has brought me from Florida line the window sill. I keep my collection of fossils, polished stones and bits of minerals in my top desk drawer.

A lawn mower drones next door. Abba's opera blares from downstairs, colliding with Neshama's radio. At the cottage there was just the water slapping against the shore. Lindsay and I used to paddle through the marsh in the late afternoons. I was supposed to look out for logs, to prevent the canoe from getting scratched or stuck in the shallow murky water. When we did get stuck, I'd watch Lindsay's arms flex as she maneuvered us off a log. Later when we swam, she'd slide her jean shorts off her narrow hips. My face flushes, the hair on my arms standing erect. Don't, Ellie.

I pick up my *Chumash* from the shelf by my desk and flip through Leviticus, searching through the section on sexual taboos and laws about lepers. I've skimmed this a zillion times before, red-faced and giggling. We don't talk about this part at school much. I leaf through the pages until I find this: *A man should not lie with a man the way he lies with a woman. It is an abomination and they should be put to death.* Leviticus 18:22. I read a few more lines. Nothing about women lying with women.

The drone of the lawn mower grows louder, buzzing inside my head. I check the Hebrew translation. Yes, *toevah*, an abomination, death. I shudder a moment and flop on the bed. How can a man lie with a man the way he does with a woman? Are people really put to death, or is it like when the Torah says to stone people who don't keep *Shabbos*? I close the book and slide it onto my bedside table. My temples throb; my whole body is feverish.

The mower shuts off and now only the sounds of traffic on Eglinton and Abba's opera waft into my room. I get down on the floor and do push-ups until I'm panting hard on the gray shag.

In the bathroom, I turn on the shower and sit in the tub. I let the water rain down cool on my head, slide down my back, like a rainstorm. I scrub my skin hard with a loofah until it sloughs off in small tawny piles.

I change into the tank top and shorts Lindsay gave me and flop down on my bed with the Toronto phone book. I scan the names until I find a M. McMullen, Lindsay's mom.

I dial the number, my pulse racing. The phone rings four times; then an answering machine picks up. "Please only leave a crucial and short message," Lindsay's mother demands. I hang up without saying a word.

What do I want to say, and how short can I make it? I dial again, gritting my teeth. "Hi, Lindsay. This is Ellie Gold, from the cottage. I was wondering if you could call me back— four eight two-two nine four two."

When my heart has calmed down, I change into my skirt and blouse and shove Lindsay's tank top and shorts back into the suitcase. I head down the street to my friend Becca's house to pick up my fish.

Becca Klein is my closest friend. She's tiny, with long brown hair and shiny eyes.

She answers the door. "Hey, you're back." She puts down her littlest brother, Yehuda, and we hug. Yehuda cries, and she picks him up again.

"Yeah, I got back yesterday."

"So, how was the cottage?"

"Good, really good. What did you do all summer?"

"Oh, you know, babysitting. Boring, but I made lots of money."

As the eldest girl of seven kids, Becca spends a lot of time looking after her younger brothers and sisters, as well as her neighbors' kids. She has more money saved than anyone I know, but she doesn't know what she's going to spend it on.

Becca puts Yehuda in a playpen, and we go upstairs to the room she shares with her two sisters.

"How are my fish?" I ask as we climb the stairs.

"Oh, well…"

"They didn't all die, did they?"

"No, only some of them." She giggles. "The kids wanted to feed them all the time. I'm really sorry."

"Don't worry about it."

Becca shows me the fish tank. Rashi, Golda Meir and Sholem Aleichem swim around the fake plants and little castle, but Ben Gurion and Hannah Senesh are gone.

"I felt so bad, I taped you this special about giant squid. It was almost interesting."

"Yeah, what's it about?"

"Oh, they stick these cameras on whales to go really deep in the ocean. And there's these really hot guys in little shorts who are scientists."

I sigh.

Becca helps me clean out the tank and I listen to her talk about the cute boys at the park.

"Were there any guys up at the cottage?" she asks.

"Um, not really."

"Oh, that's too bad."

"Yeah," I say.

BACK AT HOME we eat a late *Shabbos* dinner, the light dimming, birds still fluttering outside the windows. I remembered to keep *Shabbos* the rest of the weeks at the cottage. I recited the blessings by myself, Bubbie watching indulgently. It wasn't ever the same as home. I didn't want to leave the lake, but I've been looking forward to sitting down with Ima, Abba and Neshama, singing *Shabbos* songs.

Ima leads us in *Shalom Aleichem*, her beautiful breathy voice sending shivers down my spine. She closes her eyes and grips the table with a new intensity. When I hear her clear voice, the jigsaw pieces of my life settle back in place.

Ima blesses the *Shabbos* candles, her face hidden behind her hands. She rocks back and forth, her voice barely audible. Abba blesses the wine and the *challah* and then he leans back in his chair and chants *Eishet Chayil*, a song about a woman of valor, to Ima. She hums along with Abba, smiling. Neshama picks at a hangnail. I wriggle back and forth on the wobbly antique chair with the needlepoint cover.

When Ima became religious, she let Bubbie's canaries out of their cage. So they could be free, she explained. Bubbie found them dead in the yard, trampled, one of them missing a wing.

Ima sings only folk songs or religious music. In the morning sometimes I hear her in the kitchen singing, "We went down and wept and wept, by the water of Babylon."

"Israel was wonderful," Abba says to Neshama and me when he finishes singing. "You must see it for yourself one day, perhaps for a honeymoon." He smiles at us. Neshama looks down at her lap. My throat constricts, and I cough into my napkin.

Abba stretches back in his chair. "It's good to be home." He stands up and motions for us to stand beside him. He places his warm hands first on Neshama's head, then mine and whispers the blessing for children. "May you be like Sarah, Rachel, Rebecca and Leah." I don't hear the birds or the traffic, just Abba's words.

"Did you know," Abba asks, passing out bowls of gazpacho, "that the Talmud says God gave ten measures of beauty to the world, nine to Jerusalem and one to the rest?"

"The old city was really amazing," Ima sighs. "You have to imagine, first you're in a modern city, then the next thing you know, you're walking up this slope to Jaffa Gate."

"Your mother was so excited," Abba adds.

"There are ramparts on one side and the city below. I kept thinking of the crusaders riding up to that gate, then the Caliph of Omar, and then finally the Jews."

"You can't believe how hot it was. I've never *shvitzed* like that before in my life."

"When we got to the gate, your father knew exactly how to get to the *Kotel*—"

"I'd memorized the map on the plane."

"We went through the Armenian quarter and through Zion Square—"

"I wanted to stop at the Hurva Synagogue, but your mother wanted to go right to the *Kotel*."

"So is the wall amazing or what?" Neshama interrupts.

"Well, it was actually smaller than I expected." Ima leans her elbow on the table.

"There were soldiers everywhere."

"And the women's side is much smaller than the men's—"

"Wait," Neshama says. "Why's the women's side smaller?"

Ima shrugs. "Don't ask. Anyway, when I got to the wall, I suddenly knew exactly what I had to do."

Neshama and I exchange looks.

"I had a plan."

Neshama stops eating. I clench my napkin in my fist.

"I figured it out at the wall." Ima smiles. "First, I started to *daven*, but then—I couldn't believe it—this woman beside me started talking on her cell phone."

"Can you believe, at the Holy of Holies?" Abba adds.

"And not quietly either. In this loud Russian voice."

"Then what happened?" Neshama demands.

"Well, I found a different place by the wall, in the shade away from the woman with the cell phone, and that's when it happened." She smiles that distant smile again.

"What?"

"I had this wonderful realization. I knew exactly what I had to do."

I start to slowly shred my napkin. "Which is what?" I ask, my voice hesitant.

Ima braces her hands on the table. She takes a deep breath. "I have to help Jews be more observant."

I squeeze my napkin into a ball.

"Don't you already do that at the school?" Neshama spears spinach with her fork.

"No." Ima clutches her water glass. "It's going to be more than that. The students at school are okay. It's those other Jews, the ones who live without *Hashem*, I'm going to teach them."

Neshama swallows a mouthful of salad. "Oh," she says. She reaches for the pitcher of water and fills her glass. She drinks the whole thing down in one long gulp. "I'm glad you know what you have to do. It's good to have a plan."

"Yes," Ima says, "I want to give something back to *Hashem.*" Her eyes focus. "I want to help others."

There's a long pause. "So, what exactly are you going to *do*?" Neshama asks.

"I'm going to write a book, or maybe only a pamphlet."

"And?"

"And visitors will come for *Shabbos,*" Ima says.

"What for?" I ask.

"They'll learn," Abba replies. "They'll learn the laws and understand *Hashem.*"

"Will you help me?" Ima asks us.

I shift uncomfortably in my chair. "What will we have to do?"

"I need you to be ambassadors."

I nod uncertainly and curl my toes, looking down at my plate. Neshama has already begun her escape, and I... I push the thought away.

Ima devours another bowl of salad and two slices of corn-bread. After we clear the dishes Abba leads us in *zemirot*, our voices filling the dining room. I watch Ima sing, her head sliding slightly to the side and back, her words clear, her eyes half closed.

It makes sense that Ima would take on some sort of spiritual leadership. I just don't get why we have to be involved. I see the way Ima grasps the walls when she prays, the way she slowly rocks. Not like some who pray just to fulfill the commandment, Ima sways slowly, absorbing each prayer. She could spend an hour on a single word, letting it rise up from her toes to fill her body. In other religions she would chant loud, lead congregations and inspire them with her fervor, but not ours. Women aren't supposed to sing in public because the law of *Kol Isha*, meaning a woman's voice, can lead men to think unholy thoughts.

SATURDAY MORNING I breathe in familiar synagogue smells: old moldy books, perfume, furniture polish. I stand in the lobby and inhale deeply. I pause to peer into the men's section, and look up to the ark where the Torahs are kept in their red velvet dresses and silver crowns.

My heels click on the metal edges of the narrow linoleum staircase leading up to the women's section in the balcony. In our synagogue, men and women pray in separate sections so we won't be distracted. I take my seat next to Ima and Neshama and wave at Becca and my other friend, Esther. I survey the women, my gaze lingering over the burning red hair of Tova Suttner. She has the same rippled hair as Lindsay, thick with the weight of curls snaking down her back. I shiver and turn away.

Little girls dance over the red and emerald patterns the stained glass windows throw on the faded carpet. The men's voices rise from the main sanctuary. Ima, Neshama and I sit at the front of the balcony where we can see the sun shining on the wooden pews below.

When I open my book, the words taste like familiar food on my lips and tongue. My voice resounds with the other women's, blends in with the men's downstairs. I sway slightly from side to side.

I have been waiting all summer to pray with other people. At the cottage my voice was swallowed up by the breeze.

Ima and Neshama quietly pray beside me, mumbling the prayers under their breath. Downstairs the men race ahead, bursting into communal song. I skip ahead to quietly join in the singing. I bow to the right, left and middle, take three steps forward and three steps back as if approaching a king. All around me women chatter ("Chicken only three ninety-nine a pound.") and trade endless compliments on a new hat, a new baby. Downstairs the men sing "God is King."

When Neshama and I finish praying, we sit down to listen to the chanting of the Torah. I straighten my pale blue tube skirt, cross my ankles. The *shul* is warm, and I sweat in my white blouse. I lift my hair off the back of my neck, pull it into a loose ponytail with the elastic from my wrist.

Ima doesn't sit. She stands, swaying side to side, her face buried in her prayer book. Her blouse is modest, her heels of medium height, but everyone else is sitting.

Neshama pokes me. "What's she doing?"

I shrug.

Mrs. Bachner, who sits by the door, her hooded eyes sliding down the dresses of the women who pass by her to go to the bathroom, stares at Ima. Her thin eyebrows rise. Mrs. Bachner looks for slips showing, for blouses too open at the neck. Her eyes scrutinize children for snotty noses, for sugar cubes clutched in sweaty palms or melting in hot mouths.

Ima inhales deeply, her hands clasped tightly, her lips moving.

Neshama tucks her feet tight under her chair, shifts her hands under her knees and scrunches down in her seat. I can feel the eyes behind us bore into our backs, can hear Mrs. Bachner's *tsk-tsk*. Ima could at least stand in the back. She buries her face in her book, oblivious to the whispers behind her.

The low hum from the women's section rises to a strained buzz. I grip the velour edge of my seat. Neshama and I roll our eyes at each other, and Neshama's lip rises in a sneer.

Ima finally sits when the rabbi gives his sermon. Neshama sighs, her shoulders sinking.

I excuse myself to go to the bathroom. From inside a cubicle I hear Sari Blum say to her mother, "Who does she think she is, the messiah?"

Becca is waiting for me outside the bathroom. She grabs my hand. "What's with your Ima?"

I shrug my shoulders. "I have no idea."

Five

Before my parents were religious, they wandered, lured by the city lights.

To hear Abba and Ima talk now, my father's job as a lawyer on Bay Street was Sodom, and the Eaton's department store, where my mother worked, Gomorrah. My father was born Abraham Gold, the only son of Rosa and Yuri Gold, Holocaust survivors. My Zeyda Yuri was a diabetic, a small quiet man. Bubba Rosa was even smaller, perhaps more silent. Abba went to university and fulfilled his immigrant parents' dreams of financial and material success in their new country. Abba never moved out after he graduated, preferring to stay with his parents in their cramped apartment.

My mother, before she became religious and took on the name Chana, was Annabelle. She dropped out of the university after a year and took a job at Eaton's working in the scarf department, much to Bubbie's disgust. First Ima was into EST and Transcendental Meditation. Then she almost became a nun in a convent in Carmel, California. Finally a friend invited her to a religious dinner. "It was the music that got me," Ima always says. "I'd never sung on *Shabbos* before. Bubbie lit the candles, muttered a prayer, then we ate. At this religious dinner, people opened their hearts and thanked God for their food and the day of rest with the most beautiful songs."

Ima met Abba at that first dinner. Disillusioned with his law practice, Abba was also looking for something more.

Ima said, "Your Abba had a deep baritone voice, and when he sang he closed his eyes."

Abba says he fell in love with Ima because she wasn't only concerned with appearances. That year, before *Rosh Hashana*, she gave him two scraps of paper to put in his pockets. One said *I am but dust and ashes*, and the other *The world was created for me*.

He still keeps those crumbling pieces of paper in his wallet. "When I see them," Abba says, "I remember my own mortality and my role in life. I also think of my wife's beautiful heart and her love for *Hashem*."

Abba and Ima are now both teachers. Ima went back to school to become a preschool teacher and Abba teaches *halacha*, Jewish law, at the boy's high school. Neshama likes to refer to the material of Abba's classes as "mountains hanging from threads," zillions of Jewish laws derived from scant scriptural basis.

ON THE FIRST day back to school, the weather still humid, Neshama and I don our uniforms with our usual post-summer despair. The small- and round-collared blouse and long, navy, pleated skirt makes me look like a stork dressed in children's clothes.

Neshama and I sit in Abba's huge station wagon, the vinyl seats streaking our thighs with sweat. I slowly pull each of my knuckles until they crack. At a red light Abba turns and looks at us in the backseat.

"I want you to do the ritual washing of the hands each morning when you get up," he announces.

"Abba, we wash our hands in the morning anyway," Neshama says, staring out the window at the traffic. "That's basic hygiene."

"Yes, yes, but the prayer, you must do the prayer. I'm not talking hand scrubbing, soap, the nails. I mean ritual."

Neshama and I don't respond. We sit on opposite sides of the car, watching the traffic. Abba makes a left-hand turn.

The Torah commands us to wash our hands before we eat, which makes sense to me. Even Bubbie agrees. "Those ancient Jews had some good ideas," she likes to say. "Imagine, all that grit and sand under your nails."

Neshama and I say the prayer at home with Ima and Abba before we eat and at school where everyone lines up at the sinks in the cafeteria; otherwise we don't bother.

"Yes," Abba repeats, "you must do the ritual hand washing when you wake up." He waits for us to ask why as he slows down for the light at Lawrence Avenue.

Neshama eyes him from the backseat. She yawns. "Abba, you're not going to tell us some crazy stuff about the devil sleeping on our hands at night, are you? Because Leeba Weinstock already asked about that in Q and A, and Rabbi Lowenstein said—"

"No, it's nothing with the devil," Abba interrupts. "No devil involved. No," he pauses. "It is because sometimes during the night, we don't...we don't always have control of our bodies." Abba clears his throat. "It is possible one may"—he coughs— "touch parts of the body that are not clean. So, you should wash your hands when you wake up. Then you can be assured cleanliness."

Heat reaches up from my collar. The tips of my ears burn.

"Sounds like the devil sleeping on your hands to me," Neshama mumbles.

Abba looks at Neshama in the rearview mirror as he pulls up in front of our school. Neshama stares back while she takes off her seatbelt. "Look," he says, still staring into the mirror, "as you get older, you may come upon new temptations."

"Yes, Abba," we say quickly. "Bye Abba." We bolt out of the car.

"Unclean, my foot," Neshama says with disgust. "My body is a holy temple and I..." She throws her arms over her head dramatically, striking a pose. "I am the priestess." People walking by on the street glance our way. "Another dumb rule made up by dumb men to squash women to honor some dumb god." She goes around the back of the building to look for her friend Ruchi, leaving me blushing on the sidewalk.

Ruchi has been Neshama's best friend since kindergarten. She has stick-straight brown hair and the biggest boobs of any girl at our school. So big, Neshama says, Ruchi always has marks on her shoulders from her bra straps. Ruchi's sister, Jill, is my study partner for *Mishna* class. I usually eat lunch with her, Becca and Esther.

Ruchi is the oldest of six. We're the only family I know with only two kids and that's because Ima couldn't have any more kids after me. "Thank God," Neshama always says. "Could you imagine having a zillion brothers and sisters? I'd never get new shoes."

Ruchi has been busier than usual because her mom has been sick a lot lately. Neshama says she's had so many kids her uterus is practically hanging out of her body.

Neshama and I aren't as sexually ill-informed as most of our school friends who only glean sex education from older married sisters or cousins. Bubbie bought us several books, which we've read cover to cover. The only Sex Ed we get at school is from Mrs. Lowenstein, the rabbi's wife. She talks to us once a year about The Laws of Family Purity, which basically boil down to menstruation being *tameh*, unpure, and how you're not supposed to have sex or touch your husband when you are bleeding. Blood is always bad in Judaism, bad enough for married women to have to go dunk themselves in the *mikvah*, the ritual bath, to purify themselves after they finish menstruating. No matter how much Ima and Mrs. Lowenstein go on about what a spiritually uplifting experience the *mikvah* is, Neshama is convinced the impurity of period blood is just superstition.

Mrs. Lowenstein only visits once a year, but she keeps a box in the office where you can write her a note. You don't use your name or anything, just put some code on the note so that you can pick it up from her box later.

I sit on the front steps and get a notepad and pencil out of my bag. I tap the pencil on my knee. *I'm in love with a girl,*

I write. I look at it on the paper, feel my throat tighten. Traffic rushes by on the street. A stream of students passes up the stairs.

Does Leviticus 18:22 apply to women? I pause, biting on a fresh eraser. It breaks off in my mouth, and I chew it into rubbery bits. Finally I write, *What should I do?* I tape the edges of the note together and assign myself the number 613. Before I go to class I carefully spit a mouthful of eraser shreds into the bathroom trash bin.

AFTER SCHOOL BECCA invites me to come over to her house. "Esther is going to come too. She just wrote a new song, and she wants to play it for us."

"Oh, I just need to do something first."

"Well, I can wait for a few minutes." Becca adjusts the straps on her backpack.

"No, that's okay. I need to get home after that."

Becca frowns. "On the first day of school?"

"I'll call you," I tell her.

Becca turns to go, disappointed.

I wait a few minutes until she and Esther get a head start, then I turn down Lawrence to Lindsay's school, Havergal College. Lindsay still hasn't returned my phone messages, so I figure I'll go see her at school. She might not have heard the messages, or maybe she has her own phone line.

I pass quickly by the front entrance, with its Gothic windows and turreted stone tower, and head around the back, down a path to the playground and playing field. By the tennis courts,

I sit at a picnic table and pull Neshama's *Seventeen* magazine out of my bag.

"I didn't know you were interested in fashion," Neshama said when I asked to borrow it.

"I want to read the article on eating disorders," I lied.

She fixed me with her piercing stare, but I glared back.

I borrowed the summer issue, filled with lots of bikini pictures. Girls cavort on beaches or pose by pools, their breasts barely covered by string bikinis, their nipples pointing through the sheer tops.

The girls finally come out of the school and disperse to cars, waiting buses and down residential streets. I slip the magazine back in my bag and start to stroll around the grounds. The girls carry stylish backpacks slung over their shoulders, their long hair swinging down their backs.

If only I wasn't wearing my uniform. It's too hot for my new jeans, and I'm too embarrassed to wear my shorts in public. I tried the shorts on this morning and looked in the mirror. My legs were thin and gawky and naked-looking.

On my second rotation around the school I spot Lindsay under some elm trees in the back corner. Talking to a boy. A private school boy.

I wedge myself against the fencing of the tennis court. Lindsay stands, legs wide apart, hands on her hips. She smiles at the boy and shoves him square in the chest. He reels back against a tree. He has sandy hair and freckles across his button nose.

I bet he used to sing in a boy's choir until his voice broke. Now he probably plays rugby and is on the debating team.

His mother plays tennis at the same country club as Lindsay's mom. I watch them walk away, his hand hanging at his side, dangling close to her. His hand grazes her fingers, then slips into the gray flannel of his school pants. I bet his mother calls them *trousers* and irons them for him in the mornings.

I head home slowly, walking away from Lindsay and the guy. It's probably just a show: her liking boys. She has to cover up, like me. She'll call back soon, but not too soon. She likes me, I know she does.

I WALK BY Lindsay's school every day on my way home. I do a quick perimeter check of the building to see if she's around, then keep on going. On Thursday I almost bump into her on the front sidewalk as she comes bounding out of the heavy wood doors of the front entrance. I break into a smile when I see her long hair fluttering down her back.

"Lindsay."

She spins around. "Hi. What are you doing here?" She searches over my shoulder for someone.

"I'm just on my way home from school."

"Oh." She glances up and down the street. "So, what's up?"

"I was wondering…"

Lindsay waves at someone over my shoulder. I turn and look at the guy with the sandy hair I saw her talking to earlier in the week. She smoothes back a ripple of hair. "I have to go. It was great seeing you."

"Oh, well, maybe we can get together later."

"Sure, Ellie, whatever. I'll call you."

I smile. "That would be great."

She takes off down the street.

I slowly start walking down Avenue Road. She just doesn't want me around at her school, I can tell. I bet her mom comes home really late, and Lindsay's lonely at night. Maybe I could invite her to our house, for *Shabbos*. Yeah, right.

At the library on the way home, I head to the *World Book Encyclopedia*. When I think no one is looking I pull out *H* and walk to the very back corner and wedge myself between the stacks of books. I take a deep breath. It's just research, and not necessarily about me. I'm just reading. I open the *H* volume and flip to *homosexual*. What an ugly word, like a disease. I skim through the entry and learn that some homosexuals may be attracted to members of the same sex and the opposite sex. I also learn that young people may only be exploring with members of the same sex and are not really gay at all. I also learn that in some countries and parts of the US it's not even legal for men to be gay. It doesn't say much about women. I go back for the *L* volume, but there's nothing about lesbians. Only an entry for the Island of Lesbos: it's part of Greece and it grows vegetables. I consider looking through the card catalogue for other books, but I can't imagine checking them out, or even reading them at one of the tables. I choose a book on geology instead.

I leave the library somewhat relieved. Maybe we just experimented, maybe I'll grow up and learn to like men. Maybe.

AT THE END of the day I check Mrs. Lowenstein's box. A small envelope with the number 613 waits for me. I shove it in my pocket and scurry outside to the parking lot behind the bank next door. I lean against the brick wall, take a deep breath and rip open the envelope.

Dear Student 613, Mrs. Lowenstein writes.

Lots of girls your age get schoolgirl crushes. It's really nothing to worry about. Most girls outgrow the crushes when they leave school.

About Leviticus 18:22, you are right that it only applies to men. However, women are also prohibited from having homo-sexual experiences in the Shulchan Aruch *(20:2).*

It's important to remember that people overcome evil impulses every day. I myself sometimes feel like saying something hurtful to one of my family members or even hitting them, but, Baruch Hashem, *I have the power to control myself.*

Evil impulses are often just like a bad habit. You can change them! I think of them like biting your nails, or chewing on the ends of your hair. Reciting psalms or giving yourself a pinch when you feel yourself guided away from the path of Hashem *is a good way to stop yourself from committing a sin.*

Please write again if you need advice, or make an appoint-ment if you'd like to discuss this or any other matter in person.

Zai Gazunt, *Mrs. Rabbi Lowenstein*

I STAND ON the pavement, gnawing on my lip. Evil impulses, like wanting to yell at Abba that he's crazy or give Ima a shove when she stares endlessly out the window. I stop myself every time. But Lindsay is different.

Becca and Esther pass by me on the way out of the school.

"Hey, Ellie," Esther calls, "are you walking home?"

"Not quite yet," I manage to say. Becca looks away. All week she's been talking to me about some boy. "You're not listening," she accused me.

I push through the heavy double doors back into the school, weaving between the streams of students still exiting the building. I head up the linoleum stairs, my schoolbag bumping against my hip, back to the *beit hamidrash*, the room where we pray, meet for assemblies and have religious classes. Bookshelves line the walls, and a series of high windows over-looks Bathurst Street. In the far corner is Rabbi Lowenstein's office, a paper- and book-jumbled mess with overflowing filing cabinets and an enormous picture of the old city of Jerusalem.

I need to know exactly what the *Shulchan Aruch* says. Maybe kissing a girl is only a minor misdemeanor, and I can just wash my hands in the morning or say an extra prayer.

I scan the shelves for a copy of the *Shulchan Aruch* and slide into a chair behind a bookshelf by the back corner. I flip through the pages. Sexual relations between women are forbidden. The punishment: lashing.

The fan whirs above me, cool air swirling down over my sweaty head. A sob catches in my throat. Eyes closed, I take some deep breaths until the tears recede.

Hunching over my lap, I read Mrs. Lowenstein's note again. My head aches, and my hands leave sweaty splotches on the thin paper. *Evil impulses.* I choke back nausea and carefully hide the note in the inside pocket of my bag.

I wipe my eyes and blow my nose. Just as I am replacing the book, Rabbi Lowenstein enters the room. He is a tiny man in his early sixties with a gray beard, crinkly brown eyes and a rounded belly. Unlike the rest of our teachers, he talks, leaning back in his chair, without using his hands to accentuate his points. "Doing some homework, Ellisheva?" he asks pleasantly. He balances a stack of texts against his chest.

"Oh, just some research," I mumble, staring at my loafers.

"Very good. It's nice to see a student starting the year off right." He glances at the cover of my book. "Doesn't your father teach *halacha*?"

"Um, yes he does."

"Well, I'm happy to answer any questions you have. I'm sure your father is a great help."

I blush. "Yes, yes he is." I smile weakly and nod good-bye.

I burst out of the building and jog toward the ravine, not stopping until I reach the slope down into the trees. The dense green foliage tunnels the sun-dappled path, the maples touching overhead. Shuffling toward Bubbie's house in Forest Hill, I pass afternoon joggers in sleek running tights; moms walking their kids; elderly couples, their lapdogs yapping at the squirrels.

"Ellie, come on in." Bubbie plants an air kiss near my ear. I breathe in perfume, cigarette smoke and blue cheese. I follow her through the paneled hall past the living room with its black-and-white floral wallpaper. Bubbie's house is full of pristine white sofas and black hard-edged furniture.

She wipes her hands on the apron covering her wool slacks and turtleneck sweater. "I'm just cleaning up from my bridge group. The girls brought all this sumptuous food. Would you like some sandwich loaf?" She points to a cream cheese-covered dome of bread layered with tuna, egg and salmon.

"Is it kosher?"

"Kosher style."

"Neh."

"Here." Bubbie reaches into one of her white kitchen drawers and takes out a box of the kosher biscuits she keeps for Neshama and me.

She carefully covers the sandwich loaf, her fuchsia fingernails snared in plastic wrap.

I take a bite of biscuit. "Bubbie, these are so stale."

She shoves the box in the trash. "Well, you obviously don't come by often enough."

"I've been busy."

"Doing what?" Bubbie rummages in her enormous refrigerator. She pulls out a plate of raw vegetables.

"I'm reading about the ice age and how the glaciers carved the rock. You know, the Canadian Shield."

"Sounds great. By the way, did you ever hear from that Lindsay?"

"No...I left a message, but she hasn't returned my call."

"That's odd." Bubbie scrubs her hands at the sink. "Did you have a fight or something?"

"No, not really." I pinch my arm, squeezing until it hurts. I take a deep breath. "I wanted to ask you something—"

Bubbie interrupts, "Let me just get one thing. I'll be right back."

I hear her climbing the stairs as I wander through the kitchen. A stack of dirty china plates with pink roses waits by the sink to be washed. Silver monogrammed dessert forks dry on a dishcloth. I sit down at the kitchen table and pull out Mrs. Lowenstein's letter. *Evil impulses are often just like a bad habit.*

I used to suck my thumb and chew my fingernails. Neshama picked her scabs until they bled. I pinch my arm again, my fingernails leaving white impressions.

When I hear Bubbie coming back I ram Mrs. Lowenstein's letter in my pocket. Bubbie pulls out a chair next to me and puts a pink floral cosmetic bag on the table. She uncaps a bottle of nail polish remover and starts rubbing off the fuchsia polish. The acrid smell burns my nostrils.

"You didn't like that color?"

"I thought I'd go back to this one." She lifts a bottle of burgundy polish with the tips of her fingers. "More subdued. You wanted to ask me something?"

"Oh...I wanted to ask you...do you think people can change?" I twist the polyester edge of my skirt, lean on one elbow.

"Can you do my right hand?" Bubbie holds out the cotton swab. "What do you mean?"

I rub off the polish. "Well, just become different."

"Your mom certainly has changed," Bubbie says. "From Eaton's and her scarf collection to that convent thing and now this, this new plan." She draws burgundy polish over her thumbnail in one long stroke. "And your sister is determined to change."

"Yeah, maybe. That's not what I really mean. Besides, Neshama isn't changing that much."

"No?"

"Well, she's always wanted to be different."

"I guess so." Bubbie holds out her fingers. "Do you like this color better?"

I nod yes, chew on a hangnail.

"I'll do yours if you like," Bubbie offers.

"Neh, I don't think Abba would like it." I kiss Bubbie's cheek. "I gotta go."

"Stop by again soon."

I jog back home through the ravine.

Neshama and Ima are slowly transforming day by day, Ima into her own self-styled prophet, Neshama into Bubbie.

Lindsay wants to become a stripper instead of a private school girl.

Me, I just want to be normal.

AT HOME IMA is typing in her and Abba's office. "Hello," I call to her.

She looks up, says, "Oh, hi," and goes back to her writing.

I join Abba in the kitchen. "What's for dinner?" I ask.

"Salmon. Can you set the table?"

I nod and start pulling dishes out of the cupboard. From the corner of my eye I watch Ima pounding on her typewriter.

She pulls out the paper, reads it over, then leans forward and licks the words, one long reach of her tongue from the bottom of the page to the top. I watch her rip off a corner, put the scrap in her mouth. She rests back in her chair, chewing.

I sigh and turn back to Abba. "Can I ask you something?"

Abba starts washing small red potatoes. "Shoot."

"Jews are chosen, right?"

"Right."

"Well, what if you do something that makes you un-chosen?"

"What do you mean?"

"Well, let's say, you're like Bubbie—not religious."

"You're still chosen."

I pull out place mats from under the counter. "What if it's something worse, like...like you're a leper?"

"A leper?" Abba turns to look at me.

"Just say someone was."

"Lepers are still part of the chosen. Jewish lepers, that is."

"Okay, what about if you do something the Torah says you shouldn't do, and you do it regularly and know it's wrong?"

"You're still part of the chosen, you're just not living up to your potential. What's this all about?"

"Oh, nothing really."

We are quiet a few minutes. I finish setting the table. "Abba, do you ever find a part of the Torah you can't follow?"

"Like what?"

"Um...well, oh, forget it."

I decide to bite the inside of my cheek where no can see, and to memorize the periodic table of elements whenever I think of Lindsay. I'm not keen on psalms.

SUNDAY MORNING I get up early, and Abba drives me to the Ontario Science Centre. Other than the ravine, this is one of my favorite places.

"So, what are you going to see today?" Abba asks me.

"Ima found me these shells in Israel in the desert, in Mitzpe Ramon." I pry open the lid on the canister of sand and show him the white swirls. "I want to learn more about them."

"Shells in the desert?"

"Yeah, water used to cover everywhere, even Israel."

"Interesting," Abba says. "Do you need a ride home?"

"No, that's okay. I'm meeting Becca later." Becca has convinced me to sneak into *Dirty Dancing*. Neshama started rumors at school, hushed whispers about the bulge in Patrick Swayze's pants. Becca has been talking about it all week.

Abba drops me off, and I head up to the natural science exhibit. The shells Ima found are actually a fossil called ammonite, part of a squid-like marine animal that existed from the Paleozoic era to the end of the Cretaceous era. The Egyptians considered the fossils to be divine and called them ammonite after the God Ammon.

On the bus to the movie theater, I think about the patterns the sea would have left on the sand as it receded. The sea was there before Abraham and Sarah, before there was even the Torah. No wonder the Egyptians thought ammonite was divine. If we still prayed to the sea, loved it the way Jews loved *Hashem*, we wouldn't dump toxins in our lakes, or overfish our waters. We would pray for the sea's health and abundance. I shiver at the thought of a Divine Sea. Out the bus window, all I can see are endless concrete buildings and asphalt roads. I could take the subway all the way down to Lake Ontario, but, there too, it's just a concrete shore. All I have is where water used to be.

Up at the cottage there were hummingbirds whirring around the feeder and bluebirds cawing for peanuts. And in the lake Lindsay swam, her bare arms and legs glimmering wet, her hair alive, like rippled grass down her back. Lindsay. I bite my cheek and glance at the elements I copied onto my wrist: *Hydrogen, Helium, Lithium.*

I meet Becca at the theater at Yonge and Eglinton. She giggles with delight. I keep glancing around us nervously. We don't see anyone we know. The theater lights go down and the music comes on. Becca fixes her eyes on Patrick Swayze's swiveling hips. I keep mine on Baby's.

That night at home I lie in bed and flip through my geology book. Inside are the words I've been looking for: *molten, estuary, erosion.* Pages and pages on volcanoes spewing, landmasses slipping, tide lines ebbing. I can smell the salt of the sea, hear the bubble of lava, feel plates shifting. I imagine Lindsay expertly maneuvering her canoe. I bite my cheek: *Hydrogen, Helium, Lithium, Beryllium.*

I read until my eyelids start to close, my mind saturated with sand dunes shifting, glaciers carving paths and leaving lakes behind. Like when I swam with Lindsay, the way she teased me, the delicious scent below her ear. I bite my lip. I must want to change, become the person I was before the summer, the Ellisheva Gold whose name means "God's promise," the Ellisheva who wanted to marry the ocean, but would settle for living by it.

A car passes, the headlights flashing shadows across the wall. Yes, change. I clamp my cheek in my teeth. *Boron, Carbon, Nitrogen, Oxygen,* Lindsay. Like breathing oxygen.

BY *YOM KIPPUR*, The Day of Atonement, I know big chunks of the periodic table backward and forward. I know which elements form ionic bonds and which are least reactive. Since I can rattle helium to lithium and think about Lindsay's hips at the same time, I've decided to memorize the Latin for echinoderms instead, starting with sea stars: Sunflower Star, *Pycnopodia helianthoides*.

At *shul*, I sit between Ima and Neshama at the back of the balcony. The fans swirl warm air above us, the men's chanting rising from below. Neshama slumps in her chair, her head tipped back, silently counting the lights in the ceiling. She absently pats her growling stomach, licks her lips. Ima stands to my right, swaying, quietly mumbling prayers with the rest of the congregation. Neshama and I purposely led her to the back, just in case. She stood all of *Rosh Hashanah*, singing and swaying. She didn't sit down except for the sermon.

For once the women's section at Beth El is quiet. People are tired, hot, hungry, faint from fasting, perhaps even engaged in prayer, asking God to forgive them for their sins. Whispered greetings are the only conversation. Requests for forgiveness, the response nodded. "All the best for the New Year." "You too, have an easy fast."

Not even Mrs. Bachner notices Ima. She's busy with her daughter and her five grandchildren visiting from New York.

We stand for the confession, Neshama wiping her forehead and sighing for the zillionth time. The *shul* is always too hot on *Yom Kippur* and we're always overdressed in our new fall clothes. My tan jacket with the shoulder pads and big buttons rests in a wrinkled heap on the back of my chair. I chant, *God and God of our fathers, pardon our sins on this Day of Atonement. Forgive us the sin of disrespect for our parents. Forgive us the sin of licentiousness, unchastity, wanton looks. Forgive us the sin we committed by unclean lips.* Forgive me for holding Lindsay's salty shoulders, kissing her minty lips, wanting to stroke the curve of her waist.

My eyes jolt open, my cheeks burn. My tongue flits to the raw sore in my mouth, making me flinch. I reach my hand around to the back of my head, twist a strand of hair around my index finger and pull, the hair ripping at the roots.

"You're doing it again."

"What?"

Neshama picks a hair off my shoulder. "That thing with your hair."

"What are you talking about?"

She holds up a dark strand. "This."

"Just forget it," I whisper.

After two weeks of cheek biting my mouth was so raw, blood oozing, I decided to pull my hair out instead.

Neshama shrugs and focuses on pushing back her cuticles.

I open my book again. Please forgive me for girl lust. Please help me change. Please.

We stand for the Torah reading, a quiet chorus of women's voices. I hear Neshama on my left, and from my other side, Ima's voice, pure and clear. She sings out, her eyes closed, her hand across her heart, her voice round and whole, but breathy at the edges as if she's singing with all the air from her lungs, her chest pushing out.

Ima's voice soars louder and louder, sending shivers down my spine. In it I hear true contrition. Mrs. Zissler glances back at us, then Mrs. Blume. Mrs. Bachner turns and makes a *tsk-tsk* noise. My shoulders tense. I look at Neshama nervously.

Neshama whispers, "Ima?" Still Ima sings.

Mrs. Bachner's daughter turns around and stares. She wears a long navy suit buttoned all the way up to her chin and a high-collared white blouse, but her left eye is swollen closed. The skin is a fresh blue, almost purple, fading to green at the edges. I draw in my breath.

Ima hits a particularly high note, and Neshama finally pokes her in the ribs. Ima's eyes fly open, her voice breaking off. She looks startled.

"You're too loud," Neshama hisses.

Ima looks around as if trying to recollect where she is. "Am I?"

Neshama gives a quick nod.

Ima blushes and straightens her blouse. She tucks a strand of hair more firmly under her hat, opens her prayer book again, mumbles quietly under her breath. She sits when the rest of us do.

Throughout the Torah service, my fingers reach up to the base of my skull, trace the spot where I've been pulling at my hair. I imagine Lindsay's hands, first just touching my neck, caressing my head, and then when she pulls me closer, she tugs on my hair, her lips teasing my ear. I grip my prayer book tightly, flick my tongue against the sore in my cheek. I skim the portion, trying to follow the chanting. After the Torah service I excuse myself and go down to the bathroom.

In a bathroom stall, I lean my forehead against the plaster wall, take some deep breaths.

I hear Sari Blum whisper to her mother by the mirrors, "Mrs. Bachner's daughter is here without her husband."

"Really? Alone for *yontif*?"

"Wouldn't you be with that eye?"

On the way back I pause at the open doors of the main sanctuary. I peer into the men's section, at the sea of bobbing white backs, rows of *kippah*-clad heads. Men and boys, this is what I'm supposed to like. Danny Durshiwitz, the cantor's son, walks back my way. We used to play tag at recess even though he made speeches in class about the inner workings of the brain. I haven't seen him since we went on to high school. I should have a crush on a boy like him: tall and dark, although he isn't exactly handsome. He's too thin, and his face has broken out in crusting zits. He catches my eye, and I quickly step out of the doorway and head back upstairs.

Six

Every year at Halloween, Neshama and I begged to go trick-or-treating. We would choose costumes from the dress-up box at Bubbie's, then wait to ask Abba.

"Abba, can we please go trick-or-treating this year?" Neshama asked politely. She wore a ballet tutu with a turtleneck underneath and her thick navy school tights. I was a cat with paper ears attached to a headband, and a painted-on nose and whiskers.

We sat on the edge of the bathtub watching Abba trim his beard. Our bathroom had an old mauve toilet and matching sink. The tiling in the tub had started to drop off, dotting the tub and whoever was in it with bits of plaster. Ima had tried to make the room more inviting with mauve floral wallpaper and matching towels, but the accumulated steam and lack of a fan made the paper peel at the corners.

Abba looked at us in the reflection of the mirror. "Trick-or-treat? And have the whole community see my girls like *goyishe* children asking for candy?"

Neshama clasped her hands to her chest. "Abba, please. We'll go near Bubbie's house. No one will see us."

"Ima got to go when she was a kid," I added. "We saw the pictures. She was a princess one year, and a bride and—"

"No." Abba's voice was muffled as he trimmed the hairs near his nostrils.

"Just for half an hour? We won't eat anything until we show you."

"No." Abba put down his scissors and held the door open for us to leave.

"Just one street?"

"Out!" We scurried to the door. "I can't understand how you want to have a holiday where they throw eggs at Jews' houses."

"That was just a prank, Abba," Neshama insisted, standing in the doorway. Rabbi Abrams' house had been egged two Halloweens before.

"Like a *pogrom*." Abba's face grew red, spittle flying out of his mouth.

"You think the kids went looking for a house with a *mezuzah*?" Neshama's cheeks grew equally red, her hands coming up to enunciate her words.

Abba turned back to the mirror. "Scratch a *goy* and you get an anti-Semite," he mumbled under his breath.

"Abba! That's not true," I insisted. Mrs. Kilpatrick was my math and science teacher that year. We got to do science fair, and I built a volcano and won the prize for the school. I couldn't go to the city fair because it was on *Shabbos*.

Ima stuck her head into the hallway. She stood behind us at the entrance of the bathroom in her burgundy terry robe, her hair bound up in a towel. "What kind of *mishegas* are you filling their ears with?" Her quiet, controlled voice made me feel queasy. She pushed past us into the bathroom and locked the door behind her. "You teach our children to hate? Nu?"

I've always thought Abba was religious because of the Holocaust. I once overheard Bubbie ask Abba why he "bothered keeping all those crazy rules." Abba said that if the Jews had been more observant, the Holocaust would never have happened.

"Bullshit!" Bubbie cried. "Is that what your parents believed? No!"

Abba shrugged. "That's my opinion."

When I ask Bubbie about it later, her nostrils flared in disgust. "Ellie," she told me, "the Holocaust happened because Hitler was crazy and because no one cared a damn about the Jews. Now it's not like that. Everyone likes us, in Canada anyway. We're like kosher WASPs."

Ima was so angry with Abba she packed us up that Halloween and let us choose costumes from the dress-up box at Bubbie's. We helped Bubbie give out chocolates, and then we walked around the neighborhood looking at other children's costumes. We didn't knock on any doors, but Ima gave us kosher milk chocolate bars. We both chose to be fairies with pink tulle crinolines under our duffel coats.

"Can we go walk in the ravine?" Neshama asked.

"Ooh, too scary," Ima whispered, her eyes twinkling. She took us to the edge and we looked down into the dark trees. The wind knocked the bare dry branches together and the streetlamps cast the trees into long shadows. The light illuminated part of the path down the bush-covered slope, and the red and gold leaves covering the bushes. A breeze fluttered behind us, sending leaves skipping past our ankles and into the ravine. Chills ran up and down my arms and legs. "That's where all the ghosts live," Ima whispered into our ears, pointing down into the dark. Neshama and I shivered, stomped our feet and clung to her hands.

Neshama and I fell asleep on the white wicker couch in Bubbie's kitchen, our tummies full of chocolate and milky tea. Ima and Bubbie sat at the kitchen table, drank Kahlua, got drunk and cried.

Every year when we made our annual Halloween plea, Abba said, "Wait until the spring for Purim. Then you can dress up and eat candy 'til you're sick."

"Great," Neshama always said, her voice thick with sarcasm, "another holiday about people trying to kill the Jews. Let's cel-e-brate."

"At least the Jews didn't get killed that time," I always pointed out.

"Yeah, and in the end," Neshama added, "we slaughtered everyone instead." We didn't talk about this part of the story much at school.

ON HALLOWEEN THIS year I tell Neshama I'm going to the library after school. As soon as she's out of sight, I head toward the subway instead. On the way I stop at the drugstore to look at magazines. I scan the shelves. Fashion. Home Decorating. Sports. My eyes stop on the very back shelf, caught by the gleaming plastic cover of *Hustler*. Glancing around me,

I lift the plastic-covered corner and nudge the magazine out of its slot. A brassy blond pouts on the cover, her pointy nipples overlaid with a thin layer of black lace descending down her belly to meet in a tiny V at her crotch. The full part of her breasts juts around the thin black strips. "*Jordan, a bedroom, a video camera and you.*" My face grows hot and I quickly drop the magazine back in place. Boys, Ellie, find some boys. Pecs and abs and bulging jeans. I crouch down and look at the teen magazines. *Boys: What Every Girl Wants*, the headline of *Teen* reads. I flip through pages of advertisements and features on holiday dresses (sparkles and stars for you), the new bangs (ten easy steps) and a center section of boys. Pages and pages of shirtless, hairless, glossy boys with pecs, abs and tight jeans.

On the way to the till I spot a stack of cheap plastic witch and goblin masks. I stroke the rough edge of the plastic. Lindsay is probably dressing up for a party right now. Maybe if I walk by her house, I'll ring the doorbell and say trick-or-treat.

I buy a witch mask, the magazine and a bag of salt-and-vinegar chips and head to the subway. At Rosedale, where Lindsay lives, I get off and walk west through quiet streets of stately houses with stretches of manicured lawns. Elaborately carved jack-o'-lanterns burn on front porches. Pictures of witches hang in bay windows or sway from brass door-knockers. I pull the mask out of my bag, but it makes me feel self-conscious, so I pull my toque low over my forehead and snuggle my chin into my navy scarf. I've worn my long *shul* coat to cover my uniform.

Children scuttle down the sidewalks with their parents: preschoolers dressed like giant insects, boys as action figures, girls in princess glitter, older kids as ghoulish Halloween monsters. The streetlights flick on, casting circles on the neat shrubbery, pruned bushes and smooth driveways full of mini-vans and BMWs.

I shuffle through the dry leaves on the tree-lined boulevard. The houses, Tudor trim or old brick with leaded glass windows, loom large.

I'll knock on Lindsay's door and say, "Trick-or-treat, I just happened to be in the neighborhood." I'll lift my mask and give her a dazzling smile. She'll be just putting on her bunny costume for a school dance. Or maybe a Hawaiian outfit with a grass skirt and a bikini top. She'll say, "Ellie, I'm so glad you're here." Then she'll ask me to the dance. We'll make me a ghost costume so no one will know who I am, and we'll dance to "Stairway to Heaven." That's what Neshama says they play at the end of every school dance.

I turn the corner onto Lindsay's street, Briar Hill.

Maybe I'll just keep my mask on and ring the bell for candy, see if Lindsay recognizes me. I'd go in, but I'm wearing my school uniform with the dorky blouse.

I start counting the numbers toward her house.

Maybe I'll just wait 'til she comes outside, then I'll go talk to her. I can hide in the bushes.

Lindsay's house is brick with wooden trim. A hall light illuminates the living room and farther back, the kitchen. A Jeep is in the driveway.

I walk by without stopping.

I circle the block three times, munching on the chips. On my fourth round, the door opens and Lindsay's mom gets in her Jeep, her coat open over a tight flapper dress and fishnet stockings. Her breasts peek over the top of a heart-shaped bodice, a giant green feather sways from her head. She drives off, leaving the house totally dark.

I sigh and start walking back.

I'll go by Lindsay's school and see her there. She's probably decorating the cafeteria right now, with orange and black crepe paper, and blacking out the windows with garbage bags. I could still wear a ghost costume, or even just the mask. We could dance a fast song with lots of other girls.

I shiver on the cold deserted street and cram a handful of chips in my mouth. Ima will be wondering where I am.

On the subway back home, I flip through the teen magazine. *Ten tips to thicker eyelashes. Are your breasts too big? The secret inner passions of New Kids On The Block's Joey McIntyre.* I flip to the centerfold. Joey McIntyre stands shirtless, oiled, his chest hairless, nipples like raisins. His dark hair is combed back except for one greased piece falling over his lowered, sultry eyes. He looks mean and unhappy. The photo cuts off his legs just below the bulge of his jeans. Lindsay's nipples are more like Rosettes, bigger and pink. I twist a lock of hair behind my ear, slowly pull at it. Blood star, *Henriscula levisca.*

You might think a delicious hunk of malehood like Joey McIntyre would be all ego, but Joey is just like any other guy. He likes football, pizza, watching movies and hanging out with his friends.

But Joey has one difference. Millions of young woman swoon whenever he appears on stage.

AT HOME I flop down beside Neshama on her bed and pass her the photo of Joey McIntyre.

"Would you swoon?"

Neshama uses her nail file as a bookmark in her textbook. She studies the picture. "Cute," she says. "Very cute, but way too girly."

"Girly? I'm practically…swooning."

"You don't look like you're swooning." She flips the magazine to the cover. "And since when do you read *Teen*?"

I shrug. "Some girls in my class were talking about him." I take the magazine from her and flip back to Joey. "You're not into cute?"

Neshama stands up and nudges aside a stack of notebooks. "I want a man, a real man, not some cute little boy. Like Patrick Swayze in *Dirty Dancing*." She swivels her hips. "He was hot. Hey, wanna see something cool?"

"Sure."

She hands me a sheaf of forms.

"What's this?"

"University applications," she says.

"Wow. They're all done?"

She does a pirouette. "Yep."

"Business?"

"Uh-huh. University of Toronto and York—the first part of my magic disappearing trick.

"Now you see me"— she steps behind the closet door—
"now you don't. And"—she pops back out—"soon you won't
see me at all."

"You won't live at home next year?"

"Not if I can help it."

"You'll really need Houdini to get that kind of money."

"We'll see." She flits back down the hall.

I go into the bathroom and turn on the water. I want to
bathe in a pink-and-white chrome bathroom with shining
faucets, not in our scratched tub with the spider cracks
running through the tiles. The windowsill peels from where
the shower scalds the paint. I slide into the delicious heat,
the window steaming over, my hair floating on the surface
as if anchored by small minnows. My body is sleek, like a
seal, a slippery fish. I brush my hands over my breasts, down
my belly. If I drew close to Lindsay, our bodies would click
together like two magnets. Two skins like one. The water
washes over my head, swallowing me up. Holding my breath,
my hands slide down my flat stomach to the crease between
my legs. I press, one toe jammed in the faucet catching
the drips. I catch my breath, release my hands. Rose star,
Crossaster papposus.

Purple stars, and mottled stars, leather stars and bat stars
—I'm sick of sea stars. I sit up, water running in rivulets
down my body, my skin puckered into pruned welts, and
I pull the plug.

FRIDAY AFTER SCHOOL, Neshama and I help Ima in the kitchen for our first *Shabbos* dinner with guests.

"What're we supposed to do when they come?" I ask.

Ima looks up from the tray of chicken. "They're just here to celebrate *Shabbos*, to see a traditional dinner."

"How did you find these people?" Neshama spears a tomato with a paring knife.

"They're students from Shalom House on campus. Mr. Mordecai, who coordinates it, says they don't really know anything about being Jewish. He finds people who want to come and learn. He calls to ask how many I can seat."

"We're *seats*?" Neshama asks.

Ima ignores her. "Oh, Ellie, I almost forgot, there's a phone message for you on the counter there." She points a greasy finger at the pad of paper by the telephone. "Somebody named Mrs. McCullen called. Do you know who that is?"

I freeze, my eyes opening wide. Ima stirs the meatballs, her back toward me. "Did she say what she wanted?"

"No, you better go call her before *Shabbos*."

I try to casually walk over to the pad of paper by the phone. I lean forward and let my hair hang in front of my face. Lindsay never returned my calls, and I stopped dropping by her school.

I dial the number in Ima and Abba's office. The phone rings once before Lindsay's mom picks up.

"Hello?"

"Hi, this is Ellie Gold. I'm a friend of Lindsay's from the cottage."

"Oh, right. Hi, Ellie. I called to see if you've seen Lindsay."

"Uh, no." I slither my fingers through the coiled phone cord.

"She was supposed to go to her dad's, but she never showed up."

"I haven't seen her."

"She didn't call and say where she was or anything?"

"No, I haven't spoken with her in months."

"Oh, well if you hear from her…"

"Sure."

"Okay, thanks."

"Wait. Mrs. McMullen?"

"Yes?"

"Can you have her call me?"

"Oh, sure. I'll tell her."

I hang up the phone and sit at Ima's desk, swiveling back and forth in the chair.

"Who was that?" Ima leans in the doorway.

"Just a friend from the summer. Her mom was wondering if I'd seen her."

"You should go and shower now."

THE GUESTS STAND awkwardly in our tiny dining room, the buffet cleared of clutter, the tablecloth crisp. They watch silently as Ima leads us in *Shalom Aleichem* and blesses the candles. Abba raises his cup of wine, blesses it, then holds up the two braided loaves, shiny with egg yolk and poppy seeds. "We have two *challot* to represent the double portion of manna that fell from the sky on *Shabbos* when the Jews wandered in the desert." He blesses the loaves and rips the warm, fleshy bread into chunks, sprinkles on salt and passes them around.

Neshama's part is crooked and she's not wearing any makeup. My own hair is damp and stringy, but Ima sparkles. Her white blouse with the lace collar is crisp, her hair perfectly combed, her hands steady. Ima's limbs contract with new energy and then straighten out taut. I feel her enter a room like a slingshot, pulling herself tight, then exploding.

"Chana," Abba says, "is writing a book that may interest you young people."

Ima puts down her soup spoon, colors a bit. "It's about why Orthodox marriages are so successful."

"Did you know," Abba adds, "the Orthodox rate of divorce is practically zero?"

Ima leans forward, her hands clasped in front of her. "In the secular world people often fall in love with a person's appearance rather than their soul. You start dating someone and then realize you have different life goals. In the Orthodox world, when you are ready to get married, you are set up with someone, and you only get romantically involved after you *know* the person."

How well do I know Lindsay? I know she goes to Havergal, has no siblings. I know she likes soccer and canoeing. She wants to be a stripper. She wants to disappear.

What I really know of Lindsay is the taste of her mouth and the feel of her skin. I tug at the back of my hair.

Ima continues, "In the Orthodox world, when a young woman or man is ready to get married, and when their teacher or parent feels they are mature enough for the responsibility, they approach a go-between who sets up a date with another eligible young Jewish person. This young couple goes on a date, but they have to meet in a public place, like a hotel lobby, where other people are present. The couple is not allowed to meet in private until after the marriage." Murmuring breaks out around the table.

"Yes, I know, shocking. There's a very good reason for this. The young couple must not ever touch, not even hold hands before their marriage."

Ima smiles as the murmuring breaks into outright disbelief. "We all know," she continues, "that holding hands leads to further physical intimacy. Once you've started a physical relationship, it's difficult to objectively decide if someone is the best person for you."

And Lindsay—is she the best person for me? I think of her teasing me, the way she dared me to disappear. I shake away the thought.

Neshama and I get up to clear the table. "The reason the divorce rate is so low," Neshama hisses at me in the kitchen, "is that divorce isn't allowed."

Mrs. Bachner's daughter crawled home from New York with her five children and her black eye.

Back at the table Ima pours the tea and continues, "When I first became religiously observant I was invited to a wedding. I remember watching the bride walk down the aisle and thinking, she has never even touched the hand of the man she is going to marry! I thought it was awful, but when it was my turn, I was so in love with my *b'shert*, my one beloved, I just thought how wonderful it would be to hold his hand once we were *kallah v'chatan*, bride and groom."

I watch Ima smile at Abba, her shoulders relaxed, her hands loose on the table. That's it. I'm going to change. I want to meet a perfect stranger, talk to them about the ocean, about *Hashem* and lighting candles. My name is Ellie Gold, I'd say, and I love the sea.

Ima leads us in *zemirot* about the beauty of Shabbat and God and His commandments, and even though I am tired, my exhaustion melts away as I join in the singing, softly harmonizing with Ima.

After the guests leave, Neshama and I clean up the kitchen. "One man?" Neshama hisses. "Could you imagine only ever sleeping with one man?"

I nod and scrape plates into the garbage can.

"Wouldn't you want to test drive your spouse before you marry him? I mean, what if he's a horrible slob? What if the sex is terrible?"

"One spouse would be enough, I think. If it's your *b'shert*."

Neshama snorts. "You don't really believe that, do you? Ima wants people to get married, reproduce, follow laws God doesn't care about and that's it. That's not a way to live, that's...that's imprisonment. Not even Ima and Abba lived that way. They had a life, *then* they got married."

"Um, I guess so." I return to the table for more plates.

I'm Ellie Gold and I love the sea, but I've already pressed my hands against Lindsay's jean-clad hip, let our lips brush.

My fingers climb through my hair, twist strands around my pinky and pull. Hair coils around my fingers. I nudge the clump into the garbage with the chicken bones and greasy napkins. Slender-rayed star, *Evasterias troschelii*.

Seven

"So I hear your mother's out to convert the masses." Bubbie leans on the counter and pours Neshama and me tall glasses of orange juice.

"Only the chosen Jewish masses," Neshama points out.

I sit on a stool and stare out at the bleak November sky. A light rain drizzles over the barren trees.

"What's her plan of attack?"

"Arranged marriages."

"Aye-yah-yie," Bubbie sighs. "Unbelievable. And you, what do you think?" She taps my arm.

"Huh?"

"Your mom's dinners, how are you holding up?"

"Well, it's a little like being an unpaid caterer."

Bubbie pats my shoulder. "You just stay here and relax."

"Do you mind if we watch TV?" Neshama asks.

"Go right ahead. I taped *Days of Our Lives* for you. Do you want me to turn it on?"

Neshama slides off her stool. "No, that's okay. I don't keep *Shabbos* anymore."

"Oh, how interesting. And you?" Bubbie looks at me.

"She follows the party line," Neshama says.

"How come you're so quiet?" Bubbie asks me.

"I dunno. Just tired."

She strokes my hair. "Go, watch TV. I have to run to the store."

Bubbie's TV room is down a short flight of stairs off her kitchen. Huge windows overlook a sea of leaves, scarlet and yellow, crisp and curly on the lawn. I sink into one of the deep, white leather couches and curl up under an afghan.

In two months of trying to change myself, I now know the Latin names for thirty different kinds of sea stars and their attributes. I can do twenty push-ups without stopping and three sets of forty sit-ups. I started memorizing countries of the world *and* their capitals, from Afghanistan to Zimbabwe, but I'm not changing. In the middle of a psalm I'm thinking about Lindsay's sassy way of talking. Halfway through the periodic table I'm wondering if she'll call. When I recite countries, I'm imagining her calves by the time I get to Armenia. By Belize my hands are sliding up her knees, Bhutan her thighs, and by Brazil it's all over. I've even started to enjoy pulling out my hair. I imagine Lindsay's hands tugging, pulling me closer to her, her lips coming to kiss me again, her hands urgent and twisting in my hair. A tingle runs from the base of my skull all the way down my back to my bum.

I've done some research on gay people at the library, and being gay doesn't sound too good. Besides being an abomination according to Jewish law, all the famous gay people I've read about had tragic ends, or at least disappointing sex lives. Virginia Woolf committed suicide, Frederich the Great's young male lovers were beheaded, Oscar Wilde died in jail and Tchaikovsky got married but had a nervous collapse and left his bride after a month.

Meanwhile, Lindsay hasn't returned my calls, not even the polite one I left with her mother. She can't be out of town, and it's unlikely she's too busy. Although I've stopped by her school a zillion times, I've never run into her again. I was just her summer fling. An experiment in girl kissing, to be discarded by the fall, forgotten in the approaching doom of winter. Someone to make fun of—poor, religious Ellie. Taunt, tease and shed.

Neshama flips between channels: news, sports, a sitcom with a laugh track. "Hey, a nature show. Just your thing."

I look up, then let my cheek rest in my hands.

Neshama gasps. "Look what you've done to your hair!"

"What?" I flip up my head.

"You have a huge bald spot."

My hand reaches up to the back of my neck.

"Let me see." Neshama pushes my hand away. She traces her fingers over the bare waxy patch on my nape.

"It's nothing." I pull away from her.

Neshama flops back on the couch. "What's with you? You're starting to act like Ima." She stuffs a handful of popcorn in her mouth.

On the TV, dolphins hurtle their sleek bodies over the surface of the water. Behind them seagulls dive and soar against the sunlit sea. "I'm not like Ima, I just…"

"What?"

I sit up and examine Neshama's face. "You really want to know?"

Neshama nods, glancing back at the TV.

I squint at her. "You promise to listen?"

She nods again.

"You won't tell?"

She turns to me. "Ellie!"

"Okay." I turn sideways on the couch, resting my cheek on the slippery smooth leather. "Well, I met this…" I swallow. "This guy at the cottage that I…kinda like and now he won't talk to me—"

"What?" Neshama bolts upright, her eyebrows shooting up her forehead.

I flex my legs nervously. "I told you, there was this guy—"

"You said you had a friend, a girl."

Oh God. I squeeze my legs tighter. "I-I lied. He's a guy."

"Wait, you had a boyfriend?" Neshama slides off the couch onto the beige carpet toward me.

"Yes."

"And he wasn't Jewish?" She stares, mouth open.

"You promised to listen—"

"I'm sorry. And?"

"He won't talk to me."

Neshama crawls over to me, smiling. She leans her head next to mine. "Did you kiss, with your tongue?"

"Ness!"

"Well?"

I sigh. "Yes."

Neshama's hands drop to her sides. She stares out the window. "While I was at summer camp, you were… What's he like?"

I roll over on my back and stare at the ceiling. "Well, he's tall and a good swimmer and he taught me how to paddle—"

"Okay, but what was he *like*? Talkative, quiet?" She climbs onto the couch next to me, propping her chin in her hand.

"Well, she, I mean he…" I freeze.

Neshama narrows her eyes.

"He has great arms," I say quickly, "and really nice…skin. He…he likes to play games, tease me. He's very athletic."

She stares at me for a long moment. My heart pounds. Behind her the dolphins dive into the sea. "Did Bubbie meet him?"

"Um…well, no, she didn't. She didn't ever meet him. Don't say anything to Bubbie please. He…look, I just don't want—" I sit upright on the sofa.

"I promise—"

"Because he won't talk, and it's over anyway." I jam my hands tight under my legs to stop their fidgeting.

"You had a boyfriend," Neshama says. "One question, okay?"

I hold my breath, nod.

"Would he be worth it?"

I exhale. "Whaddya mean?"

"Well, if he's not Jewish…Ima and Abba would…He'd only be worth it if he was the most amazing, most perfect, most beautiful, sexiest, nicest guy in the world."

"Uh-huh."

"Was he the most amazing guy ever?"

I think of Lindsay licking the water glass, her tongue quivering over the rim, her eyes taunting me. "No," I whisper.

"Then, just leave it alone." She sits back on the couch and flips channels. "So, is he a good kisser?"

"Neshama!"

"I'm just asking."

"Just stop it. Okay?"

"Okay, I'm sorry."

I can feel her staring at me. I turn away and gaze out the window. A breeze ripples through the leaves, sending them upright and flitting across the lawn. "Ima is right about hand-holding."

"Pardon?"

"Hand-holding. It clouds your mind."

"Lust." Neshama pushes the *Days of Our Lives* cassette into the video machine. "Yes, clouds the mind."

I take out a geology book and try to read. I feel Neshama staring at me. I glance at her. "What?"

"Nothing." She looks away.

AS THE DAYS grow shorter and *Shabbos* starts earlier, we take our preparations to new heights to be ready on time. The guests' faces blur into a series of glasses and dark hair. Thursday nights Neshama and I vacuum and set the table; on Friday morning before school we chop vegetables and start soup. After school we scrub toilets, bake chicken. Neshama tapes the light switches to "on," and I tear toilet paper. Mia, one of the students from the first dinner, comes by early to help prepare and talk to Ima.

"Ellie," Neshama whispers from the door of the downstairs bathroom.

I put down the toilet scrubber. "What?"

"I'm trying to listen." I jerk my head in the direction of the kitchen.

Neshama leans against the doorjamb and dismisses Mia with a wave of her hand. "Same old sob story. Divorced parents, lack of spirituality in their Judaism, you know, announcing page numbers in English at the temple. All rise for the *Barchu* on page blah blah."

I stick my head out in the hall past Neshama. "She was just getting to the good part, the big confession."

"About how her dad left her mom and sob sob, they had to sell the Jag?" She parks herself on the toilet seat cover. "And, oh right, about how her boyfriend doesn't want to get married. Big surprise. Who gets married before thirty anyway?"

"Religious kids."

"It was a rhetorical question."

"Can you move?" I poke Neshama with the butt end of the toilet scrubber.

She gets off the cover. "They're all experimenters, ex-Buddhists, taking courses on 'maximizing their inner potential,' supposed 'victims' of consumerism and Western excess. Re-born Jews are *so* lost. Look at Ima," she whispers. She closes the door, squishing us together in the tiny bathroom. "But I've got a plan."

"For what?"

"Shhhh. Counterattack."

I flush the toilet and start tearing toilet paper into strips. "Attacking what?"

"The brainwashing these poor people are going through. Don't date, marry strangers you've never touched before, all that God stuff, please!"

"Yeah, so, what're you gonna do?"

Neshama grins mischievously. "We'll fill their pockets with notes—true Torah."

"What notes?"

She digs in her skirt and spreads out small scraps of paper on the toilet cover.

Embrace human rights, not Torah obligations! The Bible allows slavery. Do you?

Support equality, not superiority! Jews believe they are The Chosen People. Do you want to be part of a group that believes they're better than others?

Freedom of choice, not oppression! The Bible considers homosexuality a sin worthy of death. Do you want to be associated with a religion that denies people their sexual freedom?

I draw in a sharp breath, my shoulders contracting. I look up at Neshama. "Wow."

"Are you in?"

I hesitate. My heart beats in my chest, my hand throbbing around the toilet paper roll.

"Why did you write this one?" I hold up the note about homosexuality.

Neshama shrugs and focuses on pushing back the cuticle on her pinkie. "I dunno know. I was just thinking about all the ways Orthodox Judaism can be, you know, oppressive."

"Oh."

The doorbell rings, and she puts the notes away. "We'll stick them in their coat pockets while they're eating dessert."

"Okay."

Neshama closes the door behind her, leaving me in the tiny bathroom. I slide to the floor and lay my head on the toilet seat cover, my breath audible in the small space. From the kitchen I hear Ima singing *"Eishet Chayil mi yimsa, verehek meefeninim micarah?"* Oh, who can find a brave wife, who has no price, not even rubies?

DURING DESSERT ABBA leans back in his chair and asks the guests, "What do you think is the greatest problem in modern Judaism?"

Neshama and I exchange glances.

"The Middle-East peace conflict," one of the guests states.

"Intermarriage?"

"Anti-Semitism?"

Abba plants his fist on the table. "Those are all valid, but truly the greatest problem in my mind is," he pauses, "not enough people are waiting for *Moshiach.*"

I don't dare look at Neshama. I'm not sure whether we'd roll our eyes or merely giggle.

"But surely, you don't mean—"

"The Messiah?"

Abba thumps the table with his fist. "Only when the Messiah comes, will the other problems cease. Not only will the lamb lie down with the lion, not only will we beat our swords into ploughshares, but there will be no intermarriage, or Middle-East conflict. There will just be peace." He pauses, looking around the table. "We can help bring the Messiah by following the word of God as outlined in the Torah, and as interpreted by our revered rabbis." He looks purposely at Neshama. She stares back without blinking.

There is a moment of silence, the guests either staring at Abba or looking uncomfortably down at their hands.

Ima smiles. "How about some *zemirot*?" She stands up to get the *benchers*. Neshama excuses herself from the table. I linger another awkward moment, then get up to refill the teapot. From the kitchen, I peer down the hallway and watch Neshama shoving notes in the guests' pockets, mumbling, "crap, crap, crap," under her breath.

"That's it," she whispers to me in the kitchen. "Did you know Houdini was a rabbi's son?"

"HOLD STILL," NESHAMA says.

I sit on the mauve toilet seat cover in the upstairs bathroom. "How many more?"

"About ten." Neshama pulls the skin between my eyebrows taut and yanks out an unruly eyebrow hair.

"Ow! That's enough."

"Ellie, you can't walk around with a monobrow." She tips my chin up and pinches another hair in her shiny tweezers.

I sigh and knit my fingers tight.

"Wanna know what I'm going to ask in Q and A this week?" Her breath is warm on my cheek.

"Sure."

On Friday afternoon, all the senior girls at school have a question-and-answer period with Rabbi Lowenstein. If there are no questions, Rabbi Lowenstein gives a *drash* about the weekly Torah portion. Neshama has gotten up almost every week to ask a question about the Torah since the term began. She marches up to the lectern, plunks her notebook down and pushes her beautiful golden hair over her shoulders and announces, "I have a question." Then she plants her feet apart, flips open her notebook to a yellow highlighted page and looks directly at Rabbi Lowenstein.

Last week she marched up to the podium and said, "I would like to know why there are certain parts of the Torah that we follow and others that we deem out of date. For example…" She flipped through her notebook, one hand on her hip. "Exodus 35:2 says people who work on *Shabbos* should be put to death." Neshama blinked her big blue eyes. "What am I supposed to do about my neighbors? I mean, they aren't observant. Should I kill them?"

Last month she asked about Leviticus 21:7. "It says it is permissible to sell your daughter into slavery. Is this equivalent to arranged marriages in modern society?"

Neshama yanks out another hair, this time below my eyebrows. "You know the note I wrote, the one about how the Torah says homosexuality is a sin?"

"Y-e-a-h." I grit my teeth, my fingernails digging into my knuckles.

"Wouldn't that be great to ask in Q and A?"

I jerk away from her. "You wouldn't."

"I might. Why would you care?"

"Because...because..." My mind reels. "Think how embarrassing that would be. You want to ask Rabbi Lowenstein a question about sex? And what if...?"

"What if what?"

"If someone really was, you know..." I stand by the mirror and look at the red patch of skin between my groomed eyebrows.

"So then they'd know."

"That they were an abomination?"

"No, how stupid the Torah is."

"But they'd be so embarrassed."

"No one would know it was them."

I pause, gripping the counter. "You won't ask, will you?"

"I'm not sure."

"But it's tomorrow."

"So, I'll think about it." Neshama rinses the tweezers in the sink.

"Ask in private or wait until Mrs. Lowenstein comes." I run my fingers over the bald spot at the back of my head. New fine hairs have sprouted.

"Ellie, this is about education and power." She smoothes on lip-gloss. "Just imagine Rabbi Lowenstein trying to answer."

I sigh. "He's going to say what he always says when you ask about human rights. The Torah isn't about freedom, it's about obligation. Obligation to get married to men, to people the land of Israel, make more Jews. That's it." I put my hand on Neshama's shoulder. "Please don't ask. It'll be inappropriate."

Neshama smacks my hand off her shoulder. "Inappropriate? Who cares?" She stares at me, her eyes hard. "It's the fight. It's about saying these things in public, that the Torah is discriminatory." She stares at me a moment longer; then she slams the bathroom door behind her.

I slip to the floor, wedging myself between the toilet and the tub. I will turn bright red if she asks. I will explode with shame and anger right there in the *beit hamidrash*. And everyone will know why. Like a light from the heavens illuminating me, they will know I'm a girl kisser. They'll kick me out of school, or worse: I'll have to stay and no one will talk to me. They'll hiss "abomination" when I walk by, and I'll have to wear a pink triangle on my chest. Everyone will get married except me, and every *Yom Kippur* I will ask for forgiveness and pray to change, but I never will. Ima and Abba will ask me to move away where no one knows us, and I'll have to pretend not to be Jewish anymore. Either that or I'll have to lie and get married to some man. I shudder. And not even that will work out, and I'll be divorced and alone, and I still won't ever get to see Lindsay again. At least she gets to go to a school where they wear short kilts.

I burst out of the bathroom, grab my schoolbag and run to the ravine, heart pumping, legs churning. I slump against a tree. The air is cold, the earth barren and brown. The leaves have decomposed into wet mulch laced with frost.

I wish a volcano would magically sprout right in the middle of Toronto, a black cone erupting at Yonge and Eglinton. It would break through the asphalt, uprooting electrical poles, long shoots of lava flowing through the subway, reaching all the way out to Scarborough. The volcano would rumble below the earth's crust; then hot lava, slow and viscous like molasses, would slowly rise from the magma chamber up the pipe, *glug-glugging* over the lip of the crater. A sea of red fire would roll toward Lake Ontario, engulfing old brick houses, bungalows, century-old maples and new minivans. It would flow toward Lawrence to the North, Avenue Road to the East, the bulk flowing West, veering off-kilter to roar down the Don Valley. Whichever way it would go, I'd be swept up in a burning red roar.

"DOES ANYONE HAVE any questions?" Rabbi Lowenstein tucks his hands behind his back and paces at the front of the room. There's a long pause. I hold my breath, rooted to the chair. My arms dangle at my sides, my teeth clamping on my cheek, slowly grinding back and forth until I taste blood. My pulse stampedes through me, pounding at my temples.

No one moves. Neshama sits, arms folded over her chest, slouching, legs crossed. I look over, but she focuses on the buttons on her blouse.

Rabbi Lowenstein stops pacing. "No questions? Not even Neshama?" He smiles at her. "I like a challenge."

I hold my breath.

Neshama sits up straighter. "Well…"

"Yes?" He pauses in front of her.

Neshama quickly glances my way, then back at Reb Lowenstein. "I didn't prepare anything for this week."

I exhale a huge breath, relaxing back into my seat.

"Oh, well. Maybe you'll find something for us to think about for next week." He turns to the class. "Please take out your *Chumash*. This week's *parsha* is *Vayeshev*."

Neshama gets out her book with the other girls, languidly flipping through the pages. I gaze out at the gray sky and suck the iron-tasting blood off my cheek. My head tilts back, a wave of relief rolling over me.

I wait for Neshama on the front stairs after class. We fall into step walking down Bathurst. "Why didn't you ask any questions?"

"I was planning to."

"But?"

She zips up her jacket. "I started thinking about it, you know, what the Torah says about gay people."

"And?"

"Well, it seems so stupid. Gay people can't help being who they are, and yet they're considered abominations. And so I asked Mrs. Lowenstein."

"You did?"

"Uh-huh, and you won't believe the crap she told me. She said people could change. Can you believe that? So I started thinking, why do I even care what the Torah says? And I decided I'm not wasting my time with it anymore. Rabbi Lowenstein is super nice, and he even has good answers to some of my questions, but it's just a racist, outdated book. I mean, think about the whole Chosen People thing."

"Wait, go back to the part about, you know, the gay people." We stop at the intersection at Lawrence Avenue.

"What about them?" Neshama jams her hands into her pockets.

"You really think they can't change?"

Neshama flaps her arms against her coat. "As much as you can stop being male or female. Imagine trying to be a guy. The Torah says gay people are wrong, and they're all sinners. That makes no sense. I say, go be gay and screw the Torah. Screw it all."

"All of it?"

"Yeah, the whole thing. I'm so sick of a mean God who insists on stupid stuff like only eating animals with split hooves. How does that make you a better person? I can't believe how many generations of crazy men believe all that crap. They only do it to oppress women. Garburetors are work? Who does the cooking in all those crazy ways on *Shabbos*? Why *would* you believe any of it?"

"I…I…I don't know. Because *Shabbos* is good," I say weakly.

"So rest on *Shabbos*, but don't follow stupid rules on how to rest. It's just a book, El."

"A book inspired by God," I whisper.

Neshama scoffs. "Can you even prove that God exists? Can you?"

When I pray, the words reverberate through my chest and esophagus, filling my head. They ground me, like bull kelp, thick and bulbous, rooted to the ocean floor, yet still moving, undulating in the waves. How to explain this to Neshama?

"Anyway," Neshama says, "I only have eight more months to go of this—this charade."

"And then?"

"I'm done. With school, the skirts, the hand washing—all of it."

The wind starts to pick up. I pull my hood over my toque. We turn onto a side street.

"Neshama, can I ask you a question?"

"Yeah?"

I hesitate. "How are you going to live?"

"Whaddya mean?"

"Well, what will you do Friday nights?"

"What won't I do? Go out with friends, see movies, go dancing."

"You mean, live like Bubbie?" I cringe.

"Yeah. You did it for a summer and you survived." Neshama arches one eyebrow.

I lick my lips. "That was different," I say quietly.

Neshama laughs. "I bet."

I turn away without answering. I want to ask how she'll feel if she doesn't wake up each morning with *Hashem* on her lips, but I know she'll just laugh.

ALL THROUGH DINNER a silent rage courses through me. Judaism says I am an abomination, yet God and His commandments are supposed to be good. Mrs. Lowenstein says I can change, but I've tried and it didn't work. Neshama says God is just an idea made up by stupid men who say women can't love other women. What is God anyway? Some big guy in the sky? The creator? Creator of what? I know dinosaur bones are older than the Torah.

Ima starts singing a *zemirot*, the guests joining in. I open my mouth to sing, but the words stick in my throat, choking me. When I push the sounds past the lump and out my dry mouth, I sound off-key. I stop singing and look down at my hands.

If I'm not part of this religion, who am I anyway? Just Ellie Gold, whoever that is.

MONDAY MORNING I stand with the other girls at school, feeling tired and grumpy, to chant the morning prayers. The sky is dark and heavy, the fluorescent lights glaring over the tables. I let my gaze wander out the window to the gray street.

The girls chant, "Praised are you, Lord our God, King of the universe who made me in His image." Except I'm not in His image, not in the nicey-nice boy-likes-girl way. If I am in your image, are you gay, God? Are you?

"Praised are you God who made me a Jew," the girls chant.

Yeah, thanks a lot.

"Praised are you God who gives sight to the blind. Praised are you who clothes the naked." Does He? Not that I can see.

Thanks for making me a sinner by nature, I chant in my head to the same sing-song tune the girls use. Thanks for making me an outcast by design.

I slam my book shut. All around me the girls continue mumbling through the prayers. What good is God anyway, and what good are His stupid exclusive rules? Heat rises up my cheeks and my temples throb. When everyone rises for the *Barchu*, I slip out to the bathroom. Just to hide.

IN *MISHNA* CLASS I stare at the wall, drumming my thumbs on the table.

"Ellie?" Jill, my study partner, tries to get my attention.

"Yeah?"

"What's wrong?"

"I'm just not into this." I gesture to the book in front of us. "I don't really care what you should or shouldn't do if you're riding a camel and it's time to pray."

"But it's the *Mishna*," she whispers.

"I don't care." I cross my arms.

"What's with you?"

"Nothing," I say, too loudly. Esther and Becca look over from a table nearby.

Jill sucks in her breath. "Do you want to study alone?"

I sigh. "Yeah, maybe."

I slip out of the room when no one is looking and head back to the bathroom. In the stall I lean my head against the cold tile wall, press my fingers against my temples.

The bathroom door swings open. "Ellie?" Becca asks.

"Yeah?"

"What's wrong?"

I don't say anything.

"Can I come in?"

I unlatch the door and sniffle back some tears. "I just don't feel well. Cramps."

Becca eyes me. "That's not it, is it?"

I stare down at the floor. "I'm okay, really."

She strokes my arm. "Are you… are you in trouble?"

"No, I'm fine, really."

"If you need to talk, I'm ready to listen."

"Thanks."

She reaches up and hugs me. "Maybe if you pray really hard, *Hashem* will help you."

DURING THE *MINCHA* prayers before lunch I concentrate on a particularly vicious hangnail. In the cafeteria I skip the washing of the hands and start eating without even saying a blessing. No one notices.

After school I consider sneaking out and trying a ham sandwich or some bacon, or even just some non-kosher beef jerky, even a few gelatin-laden gummy bears. My stomach twists at the thought of *trafe* food. I just go home.

When I get into bed at night, my shoulders knotted into lumps, the *shma* rises in my head automatically as I pull up the covers and fluff my pillow.

"*Shma yisroel adonai eloheinu.*" Hear O Israel: the Lord our God.

God sucks, I think, and I stop chanting. Instead I murmur, "Yay, nature. Praise the trees. Preserve our oceans and lakes." It's not the same.

Eight

Ima's eyes grow wide and alert when the visiting cantor begins singing *Eishet Chayil*.

"*Eishet chayil mi yimsa, verahak mifninim micarah?*"

Oh, who can find a brave wife, one whose price is above rubies?

The cantor's voice resonates through the *shul*.

Ima sits on the edge of her seat and smoothes her blue suit with the braid-trimmed lapels.

"I love this song," she whispers to me. I smile at her. We're sitting in the middle of the women's section, Neshama and I on either side of Ima. The children's choir has sung some Hanukah songs, we've lit the menorah, and in a few minutes we'll eat potato *latkas*, with applesauce and sour cream, and jam-filled donuts in the synagogue basement. The rich greasy smell wafts up, making my tummy rumble.

I've been a nonbeliever for a whole month now. A whole month without praising God, except for the times when I accidentally start to mumble the prayers out of habit. Since I don't even believe in God anymore, the prayers don't count. I still keep *Shabbos* and all that because I don't want Ima or

Abba to get suspicious. When they're not looking I flick the lights on and off a few times, just to prove I don't care.

Ima starts to hum next to me. She plants her velvety pumps firmly on the floor and squeezes my hand. Neshama and I exchange glances as Ima sits up straighter and starts to sing. Don't do it, Ima, I think, but I don't want to stop her either. "*Eishet chayil mi yimsa.*" Oh, who can find a brave wife. Her voice courses through me, raw and pure, rising in volume, until she drops my hand, her eyes closing, head tilting back. She stands, stomach pushing out, shoulders back, eyes bright, too shiny. Her face is dreamy, the tension draining from her temples and tight jaw. She stands unaware, the lines of her face softening, the brim of her hat shading her face.

Neshama and I watch, paralyzed, as Ima sings louder and louder on each chorus, her eyes glazed, locked on the cantor's as if they are the only two people present, their voices dipping around the melody. Ima's voice is strong but breathy, a clear, warm soprano. If I listen closely, I can hear Bubbie's smoky rasp in Ima's singing.

I sit, hands clenched, on the edge of my seat.

Then Ima takes a huge breath and hits the high note. "*Eishet chayil mi yimsa.*" Her voice soars louder than I've ever heard, the sound more beautiful than I knew she was capable of, curling off the ceiling in perfect harmony with the cantor.

The congregation collectively holds its breath, no one moving, just listening to voices, male and female, matched.

The cantor sings more passionately, neck cords straining.

I imagine the men downstairs blushing and mumbling corrections to their straying thoughts to think of *Hashem* and not *Kol Isha*, the voice of a woman. Tears trickle down old Mrs. Zissler's wrinkled cheeks into the wool collar of her suit.

Children stop playing in the aisles and look at my mother, their eyes wide, mouths gaping.

I hear the beauty of her clear voice, and underneath I feel the pure force of her love for God.

The high note fades, the congregation moving, breathing, whispering. I hold still a moment longer, sitting up straight, letting Ima's voice resonate through me.

Mrs. Bachner turns in her seat and glares at Ima.

Over the balcony, I see Rabbi Abrams twisting his fingers in his lap. Abba stares up at the women's section, his face contracted into hard lines.

Neshama grabs my hand. "C'mon." She gathers our coats and pulls Ima, stumbling, toward the exit. Our heels clatter down the stairs.

Abba is already waiting for us outside, soft dry flakes of snow dusting his shoulders.

"I was there," Ima exclaims, pounding her fist against her patent leather purse. We stare at her. "I was there, I was there. I sang and I sang and my voice, it hit the ceiling, but I was there." Ima practically dances down the street. "I was *there*."

I shiver, wind whipping around my ankles.

Abba drapes Ima's coat around her. "Where else would you have been?"

"Oh, Avram, you don't understand." Ima paces on the pavement. "The note, the words, all reached, I...well, after I finished singing I was still in the room."

"Where else would you have been?" he asks again. He buttons up his coat, his shoulders stiff, hands rigid.

"I don't know." Ima swings her arms down. "Just not present. I've only had that once before."

"Where was that?" I ask.

"Oh," she mumbles, "it was when I was at the convent in Carmel. I was singing." Ima starts talking faster, "I was singing and singing and it was *Ave Maria*, and I hit this high note I could never get before, and my voice just rose, but it was as if I was looking down at myself and I couldn't really remember being there afterward. I couldn't remember. The nuns said I sat down and stopped singing, but I don't remember that."

"And this time?"

"I hit the high note and stayed in the room." Ima beams. We gape at her, shivering on the street, coats undone, snow falling in our hair. "Let's go back in and eat," she urges.

Abba takes her arm. "I'll make you *latkas* at home," he says and guides her down Bathurst.

THE NEXT MORNING Ima shuffles into the kitchen in her slippers and gray robe, her eyes blurry and bagged. "Good morning," she says, her voice hoarse. She pours herself a cup of tea and sits down at the table.

Abba nods, smiling weakly. When I got up this morning he was seated in the kitchen, still wearing his shirt from last night, the collar soft and creased. He stared out at the snow accumulating like thick fur over the trees and bushes, his eyes bloodshot, his beard unruly.

I unload the dishwasher, placing the glasses in the cupboard by the sink.

Ima yawns, stretches her arms over her head. "I slept a long time." Her voice cracks.

"Yes, you did." Abba rubs his eyes.

"My voice," she rasps.

Abba's sips his coffee. "You must have overdone it."

She nods, smiling. "I sang."

"Yes." Abba ducks his head. "I'll get you something for your throat." He digs in the pantry for the honey and pulls the lemon juice from the refrigerator. "Add some of that."

Ima stirs her tea. "When I sang," she croaks, "it totally filled my head, you know what I mean? I saw this color, deep purple. It turned bright blue, aqua." She cocks her head. "No, like indigo."

I stop sorting cutlery. Abba and I gaze at her.

Ima presses her hand against her breast. "And the song was pushing against my chest like it had been waiting there for years."

"That's great," Abba mutters into his coffee. He clears his throat. "I was thinking, this Friday for dinner, we'd just have our family."

Ima's smile falls. "No guests?"

"I thought it would be nice to have a rest, you know, be on vacation."

Ima wraps her hands around the mug, her smile uncertain. "If I work on my book, then I'll have more to say when the students come the following week."

"Yes," Abba says, "a good idea."

Ima picks up her tea and settles herself on the living room couch with her notebook. I stand in the kitchen, watching Abba rub his temples, his head in his hands.

ON MONDAY MORNING, the first real day of vacation, Neshama is already dressed when I come downstairs. She sits at the table next to Abba, shoveling bran flakes into her mouth.

"Where are you going so early?"

She glares at me. "To the library."

I raise my eyebrows. Abba stares out the window. Neshama puts her bowl in the dishwasher and picks up her backpack. "Bye, Abba."

He waves back, sips his coffee.

I follow her to the front hall closet. She pulls on her coat.

"I got a job for the break," she whispers.

"Where?"

"Eaton Centre, wrapping Christmas gifts."

"You did?"

She nods.

Upstairs Ima sings, "*Lo yisa goy el goy cherev.*" Nation shall not fight nation. Her voice is still raspy.

"That's going to be a long day at the library."

"You'll cover for me, right?"

I nod.

Ima comes downstairs singing, "One tin soldier rides away." Her voice is a thin scrape.

"Bye, Ima."

Ima squints at her. "Oh, have a good day."

Neshama slips out the door.

"Where was she off to?"

"Library."

Ima clears her throat, takes a breath and tries to sing. "*Avinu Malkeinu*." Her voice is deep and hoarse. She coughs and pulls snow pants out of the closet. "I can't believe my throat is still bad. Wanna help me shovel the walk?"

"No, thanks."

She zips up her ski jacket and mitts and grabs the shovel. "Jesus loves me this I know..." Her voice trickles to a slow hiss of air. She shakes her head.

I SPEND MOST of the week with Becca and Esther. We watch videos, work on a school project and try and write a new song for Esther to play on her guitar. I talk them into going down to Toronto Island, but they get sidetracked by the shopping at the harbor. I babysit for the neighbor's kids a few afternoons and use the money to buy more fossils from the museum gift shop. Becca buys me two new fish for Hanukah. We name them Nebachnezzar and Antiochus.

In the evenings, after we light the Hanukah candles, Neshama and I go to Mrs. Fidderman's to feed her cat and watch taped videos of *Days Of Our Lives*. We fast-forward through the commercials and eat popcorn on Mrs. Fidderman's floral sofa, waiting for Bo and Hope to finally reunite.

On Thursday when I come home from a trip to the science center, I make myself a cup of hot chocolate and settle on the living room sofa. Only Abba is home, swiveling back and forth on his office chair. Just as I flip open my ocean encyclopedia, the doorbell rings. I pull myself reluctantly from the sofa's deep grip. Through the peephole I see Rabbi Abrams on our doorstep, wrapped in a long black coat. Tension creeps up the back of my neck and into my jaw. He has never come to our house except when Ima invited him and his wife for *Shabbos*.

Rabbi Abrams is about forty with light brown bushy hair radiating out from his head. He has pale eyes and thin lips that disappear into his beard. When he gives a *d'var Torah*, his nostrils flare as he speaks. Neshama and I used to giggle through his sermons, watching his nose vibrate as his talk became more impassioned.

I open the door. "Please come in."

"Hi, Ellie." Rabbi Abrams steps into the hall. "I have an appointment with your father."

"Oh, I'll get him."

I knock on Abba's door. "Rabbi Abrams is here," I whisper, pushing open the door.

Abba glances at his watch. He straightens the collar of his plaid shirt. Deep circles shroud his eyes. He follows me back to the hall, rubbing his hands over his corduroys, pulling his sleeves down over the dark hairs on his wrists.

"Rabbi, so nice to see you. Please, come in." They shake hands.

"You are well?" Rabbi Abrams asks.

"*Baruch Ha'shem.*" Blessed is God.

Abba hangs up Rabbi Abrams' coat, ushers him into the office and closes the door. I sidle up to the wall, holding my breath. Did Abba make the appointment, or did Rabbi Abrams request to see Abba?

The chairs creak, and Rabbi Abrams speaks in a low voice. He mentions "Chana" and "singing." I straighten against the door. There's a pause. Rabbi Abrams speaks more loudly. "You have been a member of our congregation for many years. I value your commitment and your faith." He pauses. "I'm worried about Chana." Rabbi Abrams coughs. "Maybe if you talked to her…"

Another long pause. I slide down the wall to the gray carpet. Poor Abba.

"We want Chana to be comfortable, to be able to *daven,*" Rabbi Abrams continues.

I hear Abba drum his fingers on his desk. "I…um…well, maybe she could pray somewhere else. Perhaps her mother's synagogue."

I gawk at the door, eyes bulging. *What* is he thinking? At Bubbie's *shul,* which she hardly ever goes to, the rabbi says, "Please rise" and announces the page numbers. They recite most of the prayers in English, and a choir sings down from a balcony. No one actually prays.

Rabbi Abrams says something in Hebrew I can't make out. I hear them shifting in their chairs. I hide in the living room until he leaves.

I hear Abba talking to someone on the phone for a few minutes and then the noise of him pacing back and forth. I lie rigid in the living room, waiting to see if Ima has really been sentenced to Bubbie's reform temple. "Ellisheva," Abba calls, "can you come here a moment?" I exhale and shuffle to Abba's office, clutching my ocean encyclopedia.

Abba's eyes are hooded, his face pale. A Talmud lies open in front of him, his desk covered in papers with his neat notes. He sits, shoulders hunched, rubbing his knees. He glances at my ocean encyclopedia. "What are you reading now?"

I hold up the book.

He taps his pen on his knee. "Your sister is also studying very hard these days?"

My stomach contracts. "Yes, I think so."

"Good, good." He swivels back to his desk and glances over his papers. "I wanted to tell you I spoke with Bubbie. She says she'll be happy to have you, Neshama and your mother go to synagogue with her Saturday morning."

"To Bubbie's *shul*?"

"Yes." Abba twists his hands, pulling at his hairy knuckles.

"We have to go with her?"

"I think it best."

I sigh and lean against the wall. "Ima is going to be very sad," I whisper.

"Yes." His hand muffles his voice.

"Are you going back to Beth El?"

Abba wipes his eyes. I look away. I've never seen Abba cry, except at his parents' funerals.

"No, not right now anyway. I will *daven* at my school for a while."

The *minyan* at Abba's school is all elderly Holocaust survivors who live nearby. They mumble and rush through the prayers. There's no women's section.

Abba blows his nose and straightens his shoulders. "Your mother made a mistake, and now she needs to deal with the consequences."

My eyes narrow, and I glare at Abba. I'm not sure if I'm angry with him, or with Ima, for what she did. I turn to leave.

"Ellisheva?"

"What?" I face him.

Abba ignores my rude tone. "You'll ask your mother to go to *shul* with you and Bubbie?"

I stare at him, my mouth open. "Me?"

Abba sighs, takes off his glasses and rubs his eyes with his knuckled fist. He swallows. "You'll ask her?"

I stand at the doorway, my hands clenched, teeth bearing down on my lip. Abba's eyes brim red and watery. I nod and storm out before the tears can slip out of the corners of his eyes.

I hurl my ocean encyclopedia onto the couch and stomp to the hallway where I yank on my boots and coat. Outside, I shove the front door closed, letting it smash into the jamb with a satisfying clatter, the leaded side windows rattling in their frames. Snow has mounted on the driveway into a soft bed. I grab the shovel from the steps and start hacking a path from the front door to the driveway. The snow froths over me, offering no resistance. I chuck the shovel on the lawn and head toward the subway.

Holiday shoppers pack the subway downtown, some jovial, others tired, their faces slack. I get off at the Eaton Centre and enter the mall. Carols blare and people jostle by, carrying shopping bags. I start to sweat, clutching my hat and gloves. Stores drip with mistletoe and glittering red and green tinsel. Mothers herd eager children toward the long line waiting to meet Santa in his white Styrofoam castle. *Only seven more shopping days*, reads a giant banner.

I slowly make my way through the mall until I see Neshama at her stand. A few meters away, I stop and gawk. She wears a red and green apron over her turtleneck and skirt. A sprig of holly juts out of her headband. This is how Neshama will live: in God-less consumerism.

She waves me over. "Isn't this crazy? I've been wrapping since nine thirty." She doesn't even ask why I'm here.

She wraps a white box in Santa paper and red ribbons, expertly pulling scissors through the ribbons until they stretch out long, then furl into tight curls. She hands the package to a man in a long overcoat. "Probably lingerie for his secretary," she whispers after he leaves. "Wait a few minutes, and I'm off. Look busy talking to me about gifts and no one will come up and ask me to wrap. I tell all the men to buy jewelry. The smaller the box the bigger the love—"

"How can you stand to be in here?" I interrupt.

"*Ka-ching.*" She rubs her fingers together.

I grab her hand. "Aren't you taking this a little far?"

"Blasphemous, isn't it?"

I sigh.

At five o'clock, Neshama packs up her stand. As we walk through the mall, I tell her about Rabbi Abrams' visit and Abba's decision.

"What was he thinking? Ima hates Bubbie's *shul*." Neshama slaps her hand against the escalator handrail. "What are you going to say to her?"

"Nothing." We step onto the main floor of Eaton's.

"Hmm?" Neshama pulls me toward the makeup counter.

"I'll just invite her to come with us."

"She won't come." Neshama grabs a compact from one of the counters and starts powdering my cheeks. "This will even out your skin tone."

I grimace but let her. "When she asks why, I'll just let Abba explain."

"What a coward, making you tell Ima. Serves her right though, how weird she was."

"Yeah, but—" The scented makeup tickles my nose. Neshama steps back, avoiding the spray of my sneeze.

"But what?"

"I feel bad for her, she's going to…"

"Crumple?"

"Yeah."

Ima will deflate, melt into a puddle. She loves our *shul*. I push away Neshama's hand and check my reflection in the mirror. The makeup has caked my skin white. "You've made me look like a ghost."

A salesgirl with a perfectly made-up face leans over the counter. "Can I help you girls?"

"No, thank you," Neshama says. She turns my chin toward her. "It is a little too pale, even for you." She hands me a tissue, and I wipe off the makeup.

Outside I let the night air ruffle my open coat, the wind refreshing after the crowds and the perfume section. I follow Neshama down Yonge Street and over to Nathan Phillips Square.

"Isn't this gorgeous?" She gestures toward the colored lights and the skaters in the square across from the mall. A giant Christmas tree looms behind.

"I suppose."

Neshama sighs. "Maybe next year."

I whirl around. "You'll have Christmas?"

"Maybe," she repeats.

I shudder. "You're kidding."

"Oh, just relax, Ellie."

BUBBIE BUYS ME swim goggles for Hanukah and takes me to the women-only swim at her club. She leaves me in the empty change room while she heads out for her tennis game. I pull on my blue swimsuit, adjust the straps over my shoulders. I flex in the mirror, the curve of my biceps, the slight bulge of my shoulders visible.

The chlorine in the air tickles my nose and the tiles are cool and damp under my bare feet. The pool looks long and inviting. My new goggles suck tight against my face. An elderly woman swims in the far lane, but otherwise the pool is deserted. Holiday season. Most of Bubbie's friends are in Florida already, and she'll go down in a few weeks. I pause at the edge, glance at the ladder, and then swing my arms behind me and leap. The cool water shocks me, dissipating my anger from yesterday. I rise, gasping for air, spitting. I smile and push myself through the water. Breaststroke, like a frog. *Rana clamitans* peeping in the swamp beside the cottage.

My muscles warm up, tendons loosening, the back of my neck relaxing with each stroke. I tentatively open my eyes under water. Below me I see bubbles, tiles, pool lines, my own hands fluttering.

After a few slow lengths of breaststroke I stop, stretch my arms overhead and break into front crawl. One arm then the other. Cup and pull, breathe to the side, kick. Eyes open I can swim a straight line. I think of Ima singing in the *shul,* and a shiver runs through me, then a moment of anger, temples pulsing under the taut goggles. Just swim, Ellie. I kick harder, pulling the water past me with even more force. I will have calf muscles like Lindsay, abs like Neshama and pecs like Joey McIntyre. Energy surges through me. I break through the surface at the end of the pool, breathing hard.

Back and forth, voices echo above the water; under the surface—quiet.

AFTER THE SWIM Bubbie pulls into the parking lot at Bathurst and Lawrence. "I want to pick up some chopped liver."

"I could help you make some," I offer.

Bubbie un-clicks her seatbelt. "No, thanks. It'll make my whole house smell greasy. I'll just be a second. Do you want anything to eat?"

"No, that's okay. I'm not hungry."

"Even after all that swimming?"

I'm actually starving, but United Bakery isn't kosher. If I suddenly start eating non-kosher food, it will certainly get back to Abba and Ima. "No, thanks."

"Not even a cup of tea?"

"Okay, I guess a cup of tea."

We make our way through the ice-slick parking lot, stepping over frozen ruts and slushy puddles. The sky shadows gray, the midday light like late afternoon.

We sit at a table at the back of the restaurant, removing hats and gloves.

"So, you're joining me for *shul* this week I hear."

I stop folding my coat. "Yes."

Bubbie picks up her menu. "I heard your mother gave quite the performance the other night."

"Who told you that?"

"Your father called. You know, none of this would have happened if your parents went to a normal synagogue where women could participate. We fought for women's rights at The Shar—"

"Bubbie, Ima stood up and sang at the top of her lungs in the middle of a concert. If Abba did that it would have been wrong too."

Bubbie spreads her manicured, ringed hands on the Formica table. "Well, at least now you don't have to go back to that *shul*."

I slap my menu closed, my eyes flashing. "I *like* that *shul*. I *want* to go back." Even if I don't believe anymore, even if I can't pray. My heart hammers in my chest.

A waitress passes by, her rubber soles slapping the linoleum. Bubbie plays with the clasp on her gold bracelet, snapping it open and closed. "I didn't know you felt that way."

"Yeah, that's because you're still waiting for me to become Neshama," I mutter.

Bubbie licks her lips. "That's not true."

The waitress stops to take our order.

"Are you sure you don't want anything to eat?" Bubbie asks again.

"Bubbie, it's not kosher."

"It's so important?"

"I'm sorry," I say to the waitress, "we're not ready to order yet." I stand up and push in my chair.

"Where are you going?"

"Home."

Bubbie stands up. "Let me drive you."

I put on my coat. "If you want to."

She nods and walks to the counter for her order.

While she waits for her change, I mumble, embarrassed. "Thanks for taking me to the pool."

"You're welcome." Bubbie doesn't look at me. She tucks her scarf inside her beige coat, tightens the sash at her waist.

We drive home in silence. Bubbie's mouth twists into a grimace. She pulls up in front of the house. "Good-bye, Ellisheva."

I peck her on the cheek. "I'll see you at *shul* Saturday morning."

"Call if you decide not to come."

"Not on *Shabbos*," I say, and I slam the door of the Cadillac. I open it again. "Sorry Bubbie, about the door, I mean. And thanks for the swim. And—"

Bubbie waves. "Enough. I'll see you Saturday."

THE DOORBELL RINGS after *Shabbos* dinner just as Ima and I are clearing the table of dessert dishes. Neshama has gone to see Ruchi, and Abba has escaped to *shul*.

I peer out the frosty window into the darkness. Lindsay stands on the doorstep, chewing her lower lip, her braided hair flowing out from under a toque and over a long black coat. Nausea rises up my throat until I can taste bile in my mouth. I step back from the window a moment, my heart racing. I didn't think I'd ever see her again.

I open the door a crack. "Why are you here?" I whisper.

Lindsay puts her hands on her hips, cocks her head to the side. "I was in the neighborhood, thought I'd say hi."

"My parents are home," I hiss. "It's the Sabbath."

"Oh." Lindsay glances uncertainly behind her.

"Ellie," Ima calls, "who's there?"

"It's just a friend."

"Well, invite her inside already. It's freezing out."

I want to shove Lindsay aside, shut the door in her face. Either that, or take her in my arms. I take her coat, watch her tuck a white blouse into her blue and green kilt, smooth a navy sweater with a school crest over her hips. My teeth grind my cheek until I taste blood.

I lead Lindsay into the dining room. "This is Lindsay McMullen. And this is my mom."

"Chana Gold," Ima whispers, holding out her hand. "Please sit down. Excuse my voice, I've got a touch of laryngitis."

"Nice to meet you," Lindsay replies. "I'm sorry. I'm interrupting your dinner, aren't I?"

"No we were just cleaning up. Have you eaten?"

"I'm fine."

"Are you sure?"

"Well—"

"Let me get you something."

I sit next to Lindsay, pushing the crumbs on the tablecloth into a small mound in front of me. Lindsay looks around the dining room at the walnut china cupboard, the brass *Seder* plate hanging over the buffet.

Ima comes back with a plate of chicken, potatoes and noodle *kugel*. "So how do you two know each other?"

I clear my throat, sit on my hands. "Lindsay and her mom have the cottage next to the one Bubbie rents."

"Oh, how nice." Ima folds her hands on the tablecloth.

"Ellie taught me about the stars."

I blush, my ears burning.

"This is delicious, Mrs. Gold."

Ima smiles. "Ellie, you look flushed, are you okay?"

"Just hot." I take off my cardigan.

Lindsay swallows a mouthful of potato. "I'm sorry to just drop by. I locked myself out of my house, and my mom won't be back until really late."

And so you just decided you'd come here? It's not exactly around the block. "Don't any of your neighbors have a key?"

"They weren't home."

"Well, you're welcome to stay here for the night," Ima offers.

My eyes open wide. Stay here?

"Oh, that's okay."

"Please, it's no problem. You and Ellie can catch up."

Say no. Say your mother will be worried. Say you have to study in the morning.

"Well, if it's not too much trouble…"

Ima waves a hand. "You should call your mother, leave a message for her."

"For sure."

"Would you like some tea?" Ima asks.

"That would be great."

Ima disappears into the kitchen.

"You can't stay here," I whisper.

"Why not?"

"Are you nuts? You can't."

Ima comes back with a plate of chocolate *rugelach* and a cup of tea before I can respond. "Ellie's father made these."

Lindsay takes a bite. "Delicious."

"You're so quiet, Ellie," Ima comments.

"I'm just tired." Suddenly I feel drained, my limbs slumping into the chair.

Lindsay flicks her hair over her shoulder and flashes me a smile. I look away.

AFTER IMA AND Neshama go to bed, Lindsay and I make up the hide-a-bed in the living room.

"Your mom's really nice." She stacks the beige sofa cushions by the bookshelf.

"She likes having guests." I smooth yellow flannel sheets over the saggy mattress.

Lindsay scans the bookshelves. "So is this what you guys do Friday nights?"

"What, eat?"

"No, stay home."

Thank God she didn't come in the middle of the blessings. "It's the start of the Sabbath, so we have a big dinner."

"What if you wanted to go out?" She pulls a Hebrew book off the shelf, flips backward through the pages.

I shrug. "Not on Friday nights." I shove a pillow into a case, punching the down with my fist. "So why are you here?" My voice drops to a whisper.

Lindsay slips the book back in the shelf, rubs the dust off her hands. "I was just in the neighborhood."

I flop the pillows down on the bed and sit in the faded bluish gray armchair. "Right. You already told me that."

"I just was."

My eyebrows shoot up. "Oh, really? And what exactly were you doing here?"

Lindsay places her hands on her hips. "I was visiting friends."

"And you're really locked out?"

Lindsay turns around and pulls her vest and blouse over her head, reaching around to unhook a white lace bra.

I lean back in the armchair, stroke the worn velour nap of the armrests. The nausea in my stomach finally settles, my hands falling open at my sides.

"Of course not. I had a fight with my mom."

Tan lines crisscross Lindsay's golden back, three small plum-colored bruises etch her side. She reaches for the plaid nightgown Ima left for her and pulls it over her head. It falls all the way to her calves.

"How did you bruise your back?"

"What bruises?"

"On your side there."

Lindsay lifts the nightgown, trying to peer over her shoulder.

"There," I say pointing, resisting the urge to press my fingers into the three spots.

She probes her back, winces. "Oh, I don't know." She dismisses them with a wave of her hand.

"I have another question."

"Some things never change." Lindsay drops the night-gown, turns around and steps out of her kilt. "Yes?"

"Why did you leave the cottage without saying good-bye?"

She sits on the bed to roll off her tights. "At the end of the summer? Oh, yeah, we left a few days early because Dave had to get back to work. Of course my mom isn't seeing him anymore—"

"And you couldn't say good-bye?"

She unbraids her hair, the long waves falling over her shoulders and the open placket at the neck of the nightgown. "It was really early in the morning."

"Oh. And the phone calls?" My toes press into the hardwood floor, my teeth grate over my lip.

She smoothes her hair over her breasts. "I thought you'd be happy to see me."

I ignore the melting feeling in my chest. "You couldn't return my calls?"

Lindsay sits up in the bed, rests her elbows on her upright knees, chin in her palms. "So you're not happy to see me?"

I smack the edge of the chair with the palm of my hand. "You don't get it, do you? You can't just come here."

"I thought you wanted to see me again."

I sigh. "I do, just not here." A toilet flushes upstairs. My shoulders stiffen. "We'll talk in the morning, okay?"

Lindsay nods and yawns, stretching her arms over her head.

Upstairs I lock myself in the bathroom, where the floor doesn't squeak, and do push-ups, not the ones with your knees on the floor either, but real push-ups, three sets, until my arms ache. Lindsay, in my living room, with only a nightgown on. The new cut in my mouth bleeds. A hundred sit-ups, my back pressing into the linoleum through the thin bath mat. Ten stairs down and I could curl up behind her on the saggy sofa bed, bury my face in her hair, like Bo and Hope, finally reunited. Thirty squats, breathing fast. Plum-colored bruises like finger marks, like someone squeezed her tight.

Imagine: enough confidence to just show up at someone's house.

I spend the night twisting in my sheets, restless, rolling over. In the dim early morning light I watch the Christmas lights glowing across the street. I pull on my terrycloth robe and quietly make my way down the painted orange stairs, feeling the edges with my feet, my hands resting on the wooden banister. In the darkened kitchen I sip not-quite-steaming tea from the prepared thermos, trying to warm my hands around the white pottery mug. At seven the light timers click on, and the kitchen is suddenly bright.

In the doorway of the living room I whisper, "Lindsay?"

She mumbles and rolls over.

I tiptoe into the room, poke her shoulder. "You need to wake up."

She squints at me. "Why so early?"

I sit on the edge of the bed. "They'll be up soon." My hand snakes up to my neck to the hair growing in at the back of my head. "I...you can't come back here again."

"Oh." She sits, rubbing her eyes, looking strangely disappointed. "I was just in the neighborhood and I needed a place to go..." She stops, her voice tired. She pushes her hair out of her face, her eyes shadowed, her cheeks hollow since the summer.

"What do you mean?"

"Nothing."

"Lindsay?"

She doesn't say anything.

"I'm sorry." I don't know what else to say.

She waves a hand. "No worry. Thanks for having me."

I twist my hands. I need her to leave before I have to explain how to make kosher tea, before I have to tell Ima that she can't go to *shul* anymore.

"You really should leave, before my parents get up."

Lindsay nods. "Just a second, and I'll get ready."

"I'll walk you to the subway."

I creep upstairs and quickly get dressed. Lindsay is already by the front door putting on her boots when I come down.

We stand at the front door, pulling on our coats and hats. I reach for the door handle, anticipating the creaky hinges. Lindsay puts her hand over mine. "How about a kiss?"

I stop, stunned. "Here?"

"Sure. That's the other reason I came."

I pause. "What about—what about that guy?" My groin hums warm and wet, my arms heavy in my coat sleeves.

Lindsay steps closer to me. "He was *so* boring." She touches my hand, pushes her fingers under the cuff of my coat.

Just one kiss and I can go back to being Ellisheva Gold, observant Jew, never been kissed—at least not by a boy.

The fronts of our coats touch. Lindsay's hand slides up my arm to my cheek. She guides my face toward hers and brushes her lips against mine, soft and warm. My arms slide around her waist to clasp her to me. Her tongue probes my mouth, the kiss deepening, my knees melting.

Footsteps sound in the upstairs hallway. Lindsay and I spring apart.

"Ellie?" Ima whispers down the stairs. "Where are you going?"

"I'm just walking Lindsay to the subway. Did we wake you?"

Ima comes down in her robe. "No," she whispers, "I've been up for hours. You didn't want to stay for breakfast?"

"Oh, no, thanks." Lindsay steps toward the door, pulling on her mitts.

Ima rubs her eyes sleepily. "I got up in the middle of the night and thought, did Lindsay ever call her mom?"

"Oh, well, I'm on my way home now."

Ima's eyes narrow. "Won't she be worried?"

"Well, I'm heading there now."

"Call anyway."

"Yeah, okay, thanks for having me, Mrs. Gold. Call me, Ellie." Lindsay flashes a smile, flips her hair over her shoulder and backs out the door, closing it quickly behind her. I swing the door open to follow her.

"Ellie," Ima says.

"Yeah?" I lean back into the house.

"Go call her mother right away."

Lindsay jogs down the driveway and turns onto the street. I glance back at Ima. "Yeah, we forgot, sorry." Lindsay looks back, waves. I step back out onto the front doorstep. "I'll call later."

Ima crosses her arms. "Do it now." I watch Lindsay turn the corner, out of my sight.

"Ellisheva."

"Yeah?"

Ima licks her lips. Her eyes thin to slits. Her voice is deliberate and slow. "I don't know what you were thinking, but her mother must be sick with worry. I want you to call now."

I stop staring at the street and close the front door. "On *Shabbos*?"

"Yes."

In Ima and Abba's office I slump into the swivel chair, drop my forehead against the wooden desk. I pick up the phone and dial Lindsay's number. It rings four times and the answering machine clicks on. I don't leave a message. A sigh exits my body, exhaustion seeping into my limbs. I lay my head back down on the desk. I want to hold Lindsay's hair, and gather it in my hands like a bunch of wildflowers. I slowly get up and head into the kitchen.

BY 9:00 AM, Ima is dressed in her polka-dot silk blouse and black wool skirt. "Nu? Are we going to *shul* today or not?"

I shrug, avoiding Ima's eyes as I sit across from Neshama at the dining room table. I check the kitchen clock, pour a bowl of bran flakes. Bubbie's *shul* doesn't start until after ten. Abba hasn't shown his face yet.

Ima stares at us. "Why are you so slow this morning?"

I sigh and curl my toes. Neshama and I look at each other across the table until she kicks me.

Anger swarms through me. I swallow a mouthful of cereal and turn to Ima. "Actually we're not going to go to Beth El this morning because we told Bubbie we'd go to *shul* with her. We have lots of time still."

Ima raises her eyebrows. "With Bubbie? She never goes to *shul*."

I pour milk over my cereal. "Actually, she wanted to know if you'd come with us."

Ima snorts. "Tell her no thank you."

"Oh, come on, it'll be fun."

Ima pulls a mirror from her purse and smoothes on creamy plum lipstick. "I'm going with your father."

I bite my lip. "Um, please."

Ima looks at me. "What?"

"I really want you to come with us."

"I can't stand her *shul*. What made you think we'd go with Bubbie?"

Ima stares at me, waiting for me to respond. "Ask Abba," I mutter.

Ima leans into the hallway and calls up the stairs, "Avram, are you coming already?"

Abba comes into the kitchen. He has circles under his red eyes. "You sure you don't want to go with your mother and the girls?"

"No, thanks." Ima sucks lipstick off her teeth, checks the angle of her hat in her compact.

Neshama and I look down at our cereal bowls.

"Can I talk to you?" Abba guides her into the dining room.

Neshama and I stop eating, our ears cocked.

"What's going on?" Ima asks.

"You can't go."

"And why not?"

Abba pauses a long moment. "Rabbi Abrams and I thought it best if you didn't come back for a while."

Ima doesn't say anything. "Why?"

Another pause. "You know why."

Ima doesn't say anything for a moment. She sniffles. "What if I promise not to sing again?"

"Not this week."

I peek around the corner. Tears well in Ima's eyes. She clicks the latch on her purse open and closed.

"I'm sorry, Chana-leh, but it wasn't right what you did."

"Asshole," Neshama hisses.

"Are you going back?" Ima asks.

"No."

"Where are you going then?"

"To my school." Abba clears his throat, mumbles something I can't hear.

"Oh, I see. What about me?"

"You should go with your mother."

Ima stands up, her voice rising. "I can't pray there."

"You burned your bridges," Abba says clearly.

Neshama slams her bowl down on the counter, makes a fist at Abba through the wall.

Ima sobs. "How can I make the messiah come if I can't *daven*? I can't *daven* at my mother's *shul*."

Ima's sobbing washes out Abba's response. I want to wrap my arms around Ima, stop the sobs from her hiccuping, heaving chest.

Neshama and I don't move until we hear the front door open and Abba's footsteps fading. I peek into the living room. Ima is slumped on the couch like a deflated balloon, shoulders collapsed against the armrest, arms limp beside her.

"Ima?"

She waves a tired hand at me. "Just go with Bubbie." Her voice is a thin whisper. I glance at her splayed legs, her brown heels dangling off her stocking feet. She wipes a hand across her face, smearing her lipstick across her cheek and exposed teeth.

I hesitate at the door. "Are you okay?"

She braces her hands on the armrest, levering her torso upright a moment, then lets her shoulders sag again. She nods, mascara trickling down the side of her cheek.

"Go," she whispers, "you'll be late." She goes upstairs.

Back in the kitchen Neshama yawns, stretching her arms over her head. "I think I'll call in to work and see if I can get a shift."

"On *Shabbos*?"

Neshama clears her bowl. "It's almost Christmas; it's really busy at the mall."

"You're making me go to Bubbie's *shul* alone?"

"Just call and tell her you can't come."

I roll my eyes. "You know I don't use the phone on *Shabbos*."

"You did this morning."

"That was an emergency."

Neshama leans toward me and whispers, "A girlfriend emergency?"

I stand up from the table. "Shut up."

"That's her, isn't it? Your 'boyfriend' from the cottage."

I grab her arm, and twist the skin on the underside hard. "Just shut up."

Neshama yanks her arm away. "I'm not going to say anything—"

"Just shut the hell up!"

I shove Neshama so hard she hits the table, knocking over the garbage pail. Banana peels and crumpled napkins spill onto the floor.

I bolt from the kitchen and charge up the stairs. In my room I change into a navy velour dress I know Bubbie likes. I burst out of the house, pulling on my coat as I race down the front steps. Sunlight bouncing off the snow blinds me, but I don't care. I jog into the ravine, snow crunching under my boots, passing families with golden retrievers and chocolate labs, babies in designer snowsuits. I don't care about Ima home sniveling, or Neshama not going to *shul*, or even an entire service like a church concert with Bubbie and her perfumed, chatty friends. Lindsay kissed me, wrapped her arms around me like we did in the trees at the cottage on the flattened grass behind the sumac bushes, when her long legs wrapped around mine. Lindsay wants to kiss me.

BUBBIE'S *SHUL* IS an enormous building with carved Roman pillars, stained-glass windows and sloped seating like a concert hall. The cantor plays organ and a choir sings from a balcony above the stage.

Bubbie sits in the back row next to another woman. She kisses me on the cheek. "This is Mrs. Simon." I shake hands with the woman. "Her daughter just had a baby."

"*Mazel tov*," I whisper.

"A boy, seven pounds."

"Please rise for *The Barchu* on page three sixteen," the rabbi announces.

"That's wonderful," I say. We rise with the congregation.

Mrs. Simon thrusts photos at me. "Looks just like his grand-father, my late husband." She dabs at her eyes with a tissue.

"Bless God, the blessed one," the rabbi intones in English.

"Beautiful baby," I whisper.

"Blessed is God, the blessed one for all eternity," the congregation replies.

"Please be seated." We sit.

I flip through the mostly English prayer book. Bubbie and Mrs. Simon chat about condo prices in Florida. It's not like I want to pray anyway.

WHEN I COME home from *shul* Abba is waiting for me to eat lunch. He dishes out *cholent*, a bean and meat stew. "Where's your sister?"

"Um, I think she went to Ruchi's for lunch."

"You think?"

"I'm not sure."

"Didn't she go to *shul* with you?" His mouth folds into a tight line, his brow furrowing. He taps his fingers on the table.

I hesitate. "No, she didn't." She's out somewhere wrapping gifts for *goyishe* people and their *goyishe* holiday.

"When's she coming home?"

"Ask her yourself."

Abba stares at me. I return his gaze without flinching and dig into the spicy bean *cholent*.

AFTER LUNCH I take a cup of tea up to Ima. I open the door a crack, the light from the hall shining into her darkened room. I sit on the end of the bed. The room smells stale—like bad breath and sleeping bodies. Ima lies curled on her side in her yellow plaid nightgown.

"I brought you some tea."

"Thanks," she whispers.

"Are you sick?"

"Just tired."

I nod. Her eyes are red and shiny. "Do you want me to call Bubbie?"

She shakes her head. "I'll be fine tomorrow," Ima croaks. "Just a headache and my throat."

"Don't talk." I pat her hip. "I missed your singing this morning."

Ima tears up.

"We'll sing next *Shabbos*."

"Where?" she whispers.

"Here, we'll sing here."

"How was Bubbie's?"

"Okay. Well, lousy."

Ima makes a face. "Choir?"

I nod.

Ima comes down for the *Havdalah* ceremony that marks the end of the *Shabbos*. She melts into the couch, her face slack and pale, sudden crow's-feet at the corners of her eyes. Her voice has disappeared, as if it slid down her throat with the medicinal tea she drank, leaving her mouth open and gaping.

Neshama walks in just as Abba prepares the tray with the blue- and white-braided candle, the spice box and the wine.

"Hello, I'm sorry I'm almost late." Neshama's cheeks are rosy from the cold.

"Why weren't you here for lunch?" he asks.

"I was invited to Ruchi's."

"Oh." He eyes her outfit, a beige corduroy skirt and black sweater. Neshama crosses her arms. "Ruchi's mom is sick again. I didn't want to overdress."

Abba nods. "Let's do *Havdalah*." He lights the candle, passes it to me to hold and begins chanting, "*Hee-nai el ye-shoo-ati.*" Behold, God is my deliverance.

Ima stands to join us by the dining room table. She clears her throat, but no sound comes out. Tears edge out her eyes as she settles back into the couch.

I sigh, look at Ima and then turn back. I close my eyes and whisper along with Abba. I sniff the spice box, sip the wine and dip the candle in the cup of wine. The flame makes a *tsss* sound and *Shabbos* is over. For a moment I feel grounded, rooted in a way I haven't felt since Ima sang.

Neshama shoves me inside the office. "What did you say to him?"

"I didn't say anything."

Wrenching my arm behind my back, she forces me up against the desk. "I cover for you, you cover for me."

I try to pull away. "I'm not the one skipping out on *Shabbos*."

She squeezes my arm harder. "You cover for me, I cover for you." She raises her eyebrows.

I pause a moment, catch my breath. "Whaddya think I've been doing all week?"

We glare at each other.

She lets go of me. "Fine."

After Neshama stomps out of the office I sit down at the desk and dial Lindsay's number. My heart pulses through my chest.

"Hello?"

"Hi, it's Ellie."

"I thought you'd call earlier."

"I had to wait until...I was just busy all day."

"I tried calling but there was no answer."

"Yeah, we don't really use the phone on Saturdays."

"Oh, is it that Sabbath thing?"

"Yeah, kinda."

Wrapping the long phone cord around my hands, I start to spin, twirling the line around me, making my way from the desk over to the window.

"So was your mom angry about me not calling?" Lindsay asks.

"Neh, she forgot. When I called your mom, there wasn't any answer."

"Yeah, she slept at her boyfriend's house."

"So she didn't know you were gone?"

"Nope. So, if I can't come over to your house, can you come over to mine?"

I gulp. "Sure. When?" I unwrap myself from the phone cord, twirling back to the desk.

"Oh, whenever."

Now? Tomorrow? "I can come Monday after school."
I hold my breath.

"I'll see you then."

"Okay, bye."

I hang up and creep up the stairs to my room. I lie
down on my bed and close my eyes. The room feels like
it's spinning, like I've lost contact with the earth. I grab
my prayer book from my backpack. I shove it back without
opening it. I don't know a prayer to say when you're in
love anyway.

I close my eyes and lean back on the bed, slip a pillow
between my legs, clamp my thighs tight as a razor clam.

THE NEXT MORNING, I slip out of the house and take the bus
to the pool downtown. In the change room I keep my eyes
averted. I do ten laps, trying to keep Lindsay out of my mind.
I could just not go. Or I could just go and get my one kiss.
That'll be enough. One kiss, and maybe I'll stroke her hair.
Then I'll just walk out of her house. After that I'll be able to
concentrate. Yeah, right. I dive back in the pool and swim
another few laps. What if our teeth bump or my nose gets in
the way when we kiss? What if she wants to do something
else? I sprint the last lap in the pool.

When I get home Ima is curled up on the couch, where
she has been for the past week, except today she isn't in her
gray robe, but her nubbly pink polyester duster. Her hair
is greasy, her feet encased in threadbare wool socks, her
heels poking through. She sits on the couch, scribbling on

her writing pad, her letters jagged like scars blasted in rock. Then she methodically rips the sheets into shreds.

"Hi, Ima."

"Hey." She looks up from her pad.

"How's your voice?"

"Better."

I put down my bag. "So, are you going to school tomorrow?"

"Maybe, I don't know." Her eyes are vacant.

"This is ridiculous," I mutter.

"Pardon?"

"Nothing." I stand tapping my toes, my coat still on. Then I turn and march to the front door.

"Where are you going?" Abba appears in the hallway wearing Bubbie Rosa's purple apron with the ruffle on the bottom.

"I'll be back in five minutes."

I slam the door behind me.

Out into the freezing dark afternoon, I wrench my scarf around my neck. I slide over the icy patches all the way to the video store near the subway station to rent three of Ima's favorite old movies: *Singing In the Rain*, *Roman Holiday* and *The King and I*.

Back at home, I knock on Neshama's door.

"Come on in."

"Good, you're here." I settle on her bed.

"What do you want?"

"I need your help. What are you doing now?"

"Nothing."

"Good. We're going to kidnap Ima."

"Who's we?"

"You, me and Bubbie. Pass me the phone."

Neshama stares at me as she hands me her pink phone.

I dial Bubbie's number.

"Hello?"

"Hi, Bubbie, it's Ellie."

"Hi, dear."

"Can we come over and watch movies at your house tonight?"

"Sure."

"We're bringing Ima."

"Your mother wants to watch movies?"

"Well, she doesn't really know she wants to watch movies. We're going to try and cheer her up."

"Okay, how about eight? I'll get some ice cream."

"And one of those squeezy bottles of chocolate sauce?"

"And some Amaretto."

"Perfect. See you then."

I hang up the phone and look at Neshama. "Are you in?"

She shrugs. "Sure."

In the living room, I hand the bag of videos to Ima. "I brought you something."

She looks at the bag. "What's this?" She unfurls her limbs, sits upright on the sofa. She takes out *Roman Holiday*. "Audrey Hepburn. I haven't seen her in ages."

"I thought we could go over to Bubbie's."

She blinks back tears. "That would be great." She stands up and wraps her arms around my waist, reaches up to kiss my cheek.

"Ima?"

"Yeah?"

"You could find a new *shul*, couldn't you?"

Tears start to flow down her cheeks. "I suppose I could."

MONDAY I SNEAK out of class early to meet Lindsay. I take the subway to Rosedale and make my way through the maze of Lindsay's neighborhood. I catch up with her just before her house.

"Hi."

"Hi. You're earlier than I thought."

"Oh." I blush. "I didn't want to be late."

Lindsay turns the key in the giant oak door and guides me into a large, wood-paneled, front hall. A staircase curves up to the second floor. Light streams over a window seat surrounded by potted jade plants at the side of the hall. She starts unlacing her high, black, Doc Marten boots. I take off my coat.

"Is that your school uniform?" she snickers.

I look down at my creased pleated skirt, cringe.

"And I thought kilts were bad."

"I was going to change, but I forgot." I brush my hands down my skirt, clench them behind my back.

Lindsay reaches down to pull off her boots, her hair falling forward, revealing the delicious curve of her neck. I quickly turn away and peer through leaded-glass doors into a high-ceilinged living room. Two overstuffed sofas domi- nate the space, saggy and threadbare, surrounded by antique tables and bookshelves. Faded red drapes cover the windows at each end of the room. A water stain mars the far wall by a piano, like an oil slick on the sea.

Lindsay yanks off her boots and leaves them lying in a wet puddle by the door. "C'mon in," she says.

I follow her through the spacious hall past a dining room with an ornate crystal chandelier hanging over a long polished table. Floral wallpaper—large red roses on a cream background—covers the bottom part of the walls. Above the wallpaper, golden-edged dinner plates rest on a plate rail.

Lindsay leads me into a large kitchen, surprisingly similar to our own, but a lot bigger. The white-painted cupboards are too high, the counters the same rippled gold-flecked Formica. A faucet drips on a sink full of dirty dishes, the open door of the pantry revealing cereal boxes askew, overturned spice bottles, bags of rice and pasta spilling open.

"Yolanda comes tomorrow," Lindsay says, nudging an over-full garbage bag closer to the back door.

I lean on a stool, looking at the ample counter space. "My father would love to cook in this kitchen."

Lindsay eyes me skeptically. "It's a total time warp." She yanks open a sticky cupboard and gets two glasses. "Juice?"

I nod.

She opens the refrigerator and gets a carton from the almost barren shelves. "My mom's been trying to decide whether to renovate or sell for the past ten years."

"Oh." I sip my juice.

She grabs a box of crackers from the counter. "Want some?"

"No, thanks." I look at the dingy dishes. "So, who cooks, you or your mom?"

Lindsay opens the freezer to show me stacks of frozen dinners. "Yolanda also makes stuff for us a few times a week." She finishes her juice and stuffs a few more crackers in her mouth. "So, what do you want to do?"

I grind my teeth. "Um, I don't know."

Lindsay's eyes light up, her lips sliding into a grin. "I know."

I bite my lip, gulp down the rest of my juice.

"You like games, right?" Lindsay stands, hands on her hips, in the middle of the kitchen.

I lean against the counter. "Sure. Like, um, like dare?"

"Yeah, like dare, except this is a little different."

I crack my toes on the linoleum. "Um, sure."

Lindsay stacks our glasses on the pile in the sink. "C'mere."

I follow her back to the hallway. "Okay, here's what you do. You stand here and count to ten with your eyes closed, then you have to find me."

"Like hide-and-go-seek?"

"Yeah, kinda like that, but it's a little different."

"How so?"

Lindsay smiles. "You'll see. Just stand here." She positions me on the thin circular carpet. "Close your eyes."

I glance around at the maze of closed doors. "I'll never find you."

Lindsay steps closer to me. Her huge eyes make me hold my breath. She places a hand on my shoulder and leans toward me. "Yes, you will," she whispers.

Her voice sends tingles down my back. The skin on my legs and arms is alive. I close my eyes and start counting. *One, two, three.* I hear the stairs creaking, Lindsay's footsteps light and quick. *Four, five, six.* My heart pounds. *Seven, eight, nine.* Silence around me. *Ten.* I open my eyes, wipe my sweaty palms on my pleated skirt. I creep up the stairs, the wood groaning under my feet.

Upstairs I tiptoe down a hallway, my heart thumping. I pause at a corner, my hands clenched at my sides, press my back against the wall. Slowly I peer around to the left. Lindsay pops up in front of me, grabs my arm. "I got you."

I gasp, take a step backward.

"I got you," she giggles, her hand wrapping tight around my thin wrist.

My heart races. "I thought I was chasing you."

"And me you."

"Oh," I say. "Now what?"

"You take off a piece of clothing."

I flush, a queasy feeling rising up my torso. "Here?"

Lindsay nods.

I rub my foot up my calf, take a small step back, Lindsay still holding my arm. "What if your mom comes home?"

Lindsay leans against the wall. "She won't. She never gets here before six thirty." She licks her lips, then pulls at the sleeve of my cardigan. "It's just a sweater. Don't you want to play?"

I let her tug my sleeve over my hand. I shrug the cardigan over my shoulders, the warm wool slipping down my back, dropping around my ankles. Lindsay's eyes graze my thin white blouse, my nipples tightening against the blue satin cups of my bra.

"Okay," Lindsay says. "It's my turn to count. You hide."

"Wait."

"What?"

My hand reaches out to the hem of Lindsay's kilt, tugging at the edge. "I found you too," I whisper. I can't believe what I just said.

Lindsay frowns. "So you think I should take off something too?"

I cross my legs, press one shoulder up to my ear. "Yes," I say, my voice barely audible. I look down at her stocking feet.

"Fair enough." She smiles and starts pulling off her vest. Then she stops, raises one eyebrow. Her hand slides down her blouse, over her kilt, snakes up one bare thigh. My mouth drops open as she hooks a thumb under her panties. She wiggles them, white and lacy, down her legs, and lets them drop down to her ankles. She calmly steps out of them and shoves them in her cardigan pocket. I draw in a deep breath and lean against the wall.

"So I can tag you and you can tag me?" I ask, swallowing.

"If you can find me." Lindsay's fingers trace the bony ridge of my now naked wrist.

"Is this hide-and-go-seek or tag?"

"Both—neither." She smiles. "Whatever you want it to be." She slips her fingers between mine, her palm pressed tight against mine.

Lindsay cocks her head to the side, a finger at the corner of her mouth. "You'll figure it out—you're smart." She tightens her grip on my hand, pulling me toward her. "Catch me if you can," she whispers. Then she pulls away, her hair streaming loose behind her. I lunge down the hallway, my fingers grazing her waist by the open door of the bathroom.

Lindsay stands, laughing. "Okay, you got me," she says.

Suddenly I'm embarrassed to have caught her so fast, my face crimson. "I…I…You don't have to take off anything. I just, I just want to…," my lips fumble. Lindsay waits for me. "I want to touch your hair," I blurt. Heat climbs up my cheek. I stare down at the carpet.

She stops laughing. "So touch it."

I breathe in deep, pausing a moment before stepping closer to her. I run my fingers tentatively over the top of her head, let them trail down the long soft strands to her shoulders. Lindsay watches me curiously, her huge eyes fixed on mine. I gather a thick lock of her hair and bring it up to my face. "I love your hair," I whisper. It smells like the day we lay in the wild grass in the field with the sumac. I close my eyes, inhaling her scent, burying my fingers in the strawberry-blond waves until I feel her fingers on my hip, edging my blouse out of my uniform skirt.

My eyes fly open. "You didn't tag me back."

She spreads her cool hands over my bare narrow stomach. "I'm tagging you now," she says. Her hands reach up to my breasts.

I gasp, my nipples stabbing into the palms of her hands.

Our fingers work the buttons on our blouses, pushing plastic through the cotton holes. Lindsay wears a white bra, lace petals around her puckered nipples. I hold the weight of her breast in my hand, heavy and white, feel its round bottom curve, watch the nipple crease tighter under my gaze.

Lindsay sighs. "Tag me," she murmurs, "please tag me."

Nine

Nose deep in the sofa, my cheekbone rests against Lindsay's warm shoulder, our legs entwined.

"El?" Lindsay nudges me.

"Hmm." I bury myself deeper in the velvet cushions.

"You need to go."

I sigh. "Time?"

"Five thirty."

I slowly get up from the sofa, twist my school skirt straight, pick panties from my bum.

I've gone to Lindsay's every Tuesday and Thursday for the past three months. I haven't been to the Science Center since the winter break, and Becca has almost given up on me. I try and see her on the weekends or call in the evenings, but I know she is hurt. She hangs out with Esther most of the time now.

Lindsay and I spend the afternoons watching TV in the den on deep white couches, the blinds drawn. With a velvety blanket over our laps, our fingers stroke the edge of a hem, a knee, our breath heavy and warm. Hands travel up smooth white tights to cotton underpants, the sharp gasp as fingers delve between warm wet folds, legs splayed, breath muted. Mouths hang slack, too busy breathing to kiss.

Lindsay watches me comb my hair. "What do you tell your parents?"

"Library."

"And they believe you?"

I nod.

"Mine wouldn't."

"I'm the good girl. Besides…"

"What?"

Ima sits in her office every evening, scribbling. Abba spends long hours at school, working on an article. "They watch Neshama more."

"Is she as bad as you?" Lindsay grins in the dark.

I tuck in my blouse. "She has other agendas."

"Like?"

"Money and school."

"And you?"

I almost say "love," the word on the edge of my lips. "I have, I have other…"

"More physical concerns?" Lindsay reaches out and strokes my knee.

"What's your agenda?" Say love, say it's love. I stop dressing and watch her.

Lindsay stretches lazily on the couch. "Oh, I don't know. Stripping." She grins.

I sulk into the couch.

"What's wrong?"

"Oh. Nothing."

Lindsay walks me to the subway. It's already dark outside, the night air damp, the streetlights casting pools on the snow. We walk silently through the quiet streets.

"What do you think your parents would do if they found out?" she asks.

I think about this for a moment. "Cry."

"Cry?"

I nod slowly. "Yours?"

Lindsay shrugs. "I've never thought about it."

Every night I lie in bed worrying, what if they find out? I buy more teen magazines and plaster my walls with stupid glossy centerfolds. I even buy a Patrick Swayze *Dirty Dancing* poster. If we were still going to Beth El, Mrs. Bachner would sniff me out, her hooded eyes staring into me until she figured out what it was. "Oh, that Ellie Gold, she walks different than she used to."

I've started going swimming on days I don't go to Lindsay's. Another lie to Abba: I tell him I only go to the women's swim, which isn't true. Every second week I think, I won't go back to her, I just won't. But I do. January and February has been full of slow, sweet kisses and crawling fingers.

I say good-bye to Lindsay at the subway entrance.

"Where are you going now?" I ask.

"Just out."

"Oh."

"Come by next week."

"Okay."

"See you."

"Yeah, see you." I try to keep disappointment out of my voice.

I pause at the subway entrance to watch Lindsay. She rounds the corner to Yonge Street and heads down the block, away from her house. At the crosswalk she takes off her toque, shakes out her hair. She extends one arm, her gloved thumb lifted away from her closed fist.

Eyes open wide, toes curling in my boots, I press myself against the wall of the station. Cars pass, throwing slush into the snowbank under the streetlights. People pass in chic over-coats carrying briefcases or shopping bags. I hold my breath, shivering. A Corvette slows down, and Lindsay turns her head to follow it, her stance wide. She runs her hands through her hair, her huge eyes staring at the car. It slows down at the corner near the subway. I sneak behind the entrance, my hand over my mouth. My knees lock and my arms are rigid as she leans into the car window. A sick feeling rises up my throat as she opens the door and slides in. I catch a glimpse of a guy in a baseball cap.

I stare at the departed car, the snow falling over me. My breath melts on my scarf, the wet wool chafing my chin. A wave of warm stale air hits my nostrils as I push my way into the subway.

My hands come up in the air and slap down against my legs. She dared me to hitch at the cottage. The time she came to my house, the bruises on her side. She just happened to be in the neighborhood. Who drove her then? When her mom called that time, was she in some guy's car, with his hand between her legs? My teeth chattering,

I step onto the northbound train and slump into a seat, staring straight ahead. Anger slowly seethes inside me, my fists forming tight bundles at my sides. This is what I get for being with a girl. Tears start to well up in my eyes. I squeeze my lids tight, but the tears edge their way down my cheeks. A woman taps me on the shoulder, her face kindly. "Have a tissue, dear."

"Thank you," I whisper.

I look up and realize we're already at York Mills. I get off and head back south.

At home I find Neshama upstairs in her room. I stand at the doorway, watching her as she takes her music boxes off the shelf, wraps them in tissue paper and places them in a carton.

"Can I talk to you?"

She whirls around. "I'm busy now."

I lean against the doorjamb. "Are you going some-where?"

"No." She doesn't look at me.

"Then why are you packing?"

"I'm not. I'm cleaning."

She fills a box with teddy bears from her bed.

I sit down at her surprisingly neat desk. "Even Mr. Bear has to go?"

"Yep." She chucks him into the box.

I lean over and pull out the little blue bear Bubba Rosa gave her and tuck it under my arm.

"Can you close the door?" she asks.

"Me in or out?"

"Doesn't matter."

I quietly close the door, leaving her alone.

ON SATURDAY MORNING, Ima comes into the kitchen wearing her navy suit and matching hat. Her hair is neatly waved, her eye makeup carefully applied. "Anyone want to come to *shul* with me?"

Abba sips his coffee. "Where are you off to this time?"

"Same as last week."

Ima eats a croissant, careful not to smudge her lipstick. "Wanna come?" she asks hopefully. "I think you'd like it."

"Oh, I think I'll just head to school." Abba puts his coffee mug in the dishwasher.

She shrugs and pops the rest of the croissant in her mouth.

For the past couple of months, Ima has been trying different *shuls* all over the city. The day after our movie marathon, she went back to work with circles under her eyes, her voice still weak, but I haven't heard her sing in months. Not at *Shabbos*, not even in the shower. She's been quiet, calm, back to staring out the kitchen window at the pillows of snow covering our backyard.

"How about you girls?" Abba asks.

"I'm going with Ruchi," Neshama says.

"Ellie?"

I hesitate. I haven't really spoken to Abba since Rabbi Abrams' visit.

"You can come with me and Ruchi."

"Well, um, yeah, maybe I'll do that."

I went to *shul* with Bubbie until she left for Florida. Since then Neshama and I've been doing this routine with Ima and Abba. Once they leave, I spend the mornings at home reading, or wandering through the snow-covered ravine. Saturday morning has opened into a gray time of indecision. Bubbie's been back from Florida for a few weeks, but she made it clear she wasn't interested in attending every week.

Ima and Abba put on their coats. "See you girls at lunch. Oh, I almost forgot to tell you," Abba says. "We'll be having guests again starting next week." He smiles at us and closes the door behind him.

"No!" Neshama wails.

I drop into my chair. "Great. Gold Family Catering resurrected." No one has said anything about Ima's book, or the dinners, for months.

"Forget that. I'm doing as little as possible." Neshama pulls her blond curls into a plastic butterfly clip, fluffing out her bangs. "So, what are you going to do today?"

"I dunno. You?"

"I'm going to the library. Wanna come?"

"Neh."

I wander, picking up books and putting them down. I think about Lindsay laughing next to some guy in a car, and shudder. In the office I sit down at the desk and look at the phone. The receiver is smooth in my hand. Lindsay picks up after the second ring.

"Hello?"

"Hi, it's me."

"I thought you didn't use the phone on Saturday."

"I don't, but, well, what are you doing now?"

"Watching cartoons."

"Can I come over?"

"On your Sabbath? Is everything okay?"

"Yeah…I just want to talk to you."

"Sure, come over. It's just me and my Wheaties."

Outside I find myself walking toward the *shul* instead of to the subway. The air is mild for March, but wet and gritty. Blackened snow banks the sidewalks and puddles of gray slush melt at the curb. An overcast sky hangs low, the air stagnant.

On Bathurst I watch families struggle over icy pavement to go to their *shuls*, the girls in long coats, following their black-hatted Abbas. I could walk into any one of those *shuls* where no one would know me.

I slip into the lobby of our *shul* just for a moment, just to inhale the scent of damp books and furniture polish. The bottom of my skirt clings in a wet ring to my tights. I pull off my toque, my hair lifting out in a halo of static.

When I peer into the main sanctuary a wave of nostalgia rushes over me so strong that I need to lean against the doorway. The congregation sings *Adonai Melach*, the male voices low and sonorous, filling the building. Just for a second. I'll just listen a moment. I brush a wisp of hair out of my eye, catching a tear at the same time.

The women's voices draw me up the stairs to the balcony. In the stairwell outside the door to the women's section I grip the banister, listening to the women's voices surging toward the high ceiling. If Ima were here her voice would be the loudest, the most passionate. Tears well in my eyes and threaten to spill out. I hold my breath and count to ten. When I open my mouth to breathe, the song rushes out of my mouth, "*Adonai Melach*." The Lord is King.

A woman comes up the stairs behind me. I'm blocking the door, but I'm too embarrassed to say that I'm just going to pray in the hallway, so I go in and stand near the door. Only for a moment.

"*Adonai yimlokh l'olam va'ed.*" The Lord Shall be King Forever.

I tip my head up, let my eyes close, my voice scrolling into the desire to be heard. You are Our Father, Our King. I feel like a stack of drawers that have been off their tracks, the slots finally shuttling back into their dresser grooves. I've prayed this way every Saturday morning my entire life, except for the past two months. I don't care that I don't believe in Our Father, Our King anymore, I just want to grow up and be like other women with their husbands and babies and their toddlers leaning against their skirted legs. I want to be part of this kingdom.

The cantor continues chanting the prayer. When I open my eyes Mrs. Bachner is staring at me, her eyes raking over my messy hair and damp skirt. I stare back, narrowing my eyes at her until she turns away. I swallow the bitter bile in my throat and bolt down the stairs, not minding the slapping of my boots against the metal edges of the steps.

I run to the subway, my feet sliding on the slick side-walks. Our Father, Our King, who creates mean rules.

Our Father, Our King, an idea thought up by dumb men, and women stupid enough to follow them, but not me.

When I get off at Rosedale, the snow has turned to fat drops of sleety rain. The lawns are brown and patchy, the trees bare, the bushes still settled with white hats of snow, like old men.

Lindsay answers the door, wearing white flannel pajamas with small pink bunnies. "You're soaking."

"It's really gross out." I run my hand over my wet hair. She takes my coat, and I roll off my damp tights. The backs of my legs are red and cold from my soaking skirt.

"You must be freezing. I'll get you something to wear. Or…"

"What?"

She smiles. "Follow me."

She leads me up the stairs to her mother's room. The walls are painted peach with white trim. Crumpled clothing and bags of dry cleaning lie scattered over a four-poster bed and a stuffed chair. I follow her through the gloomy room into a huge, blue and gold bathroom. Unlike the rest of Lindsay's paint-peeling, creaking house, the bathroom is new, with navy fixtures and gold trim. A deep blue bathtub dominates the far end of the bathroom. Lindsay turns on the hot water and pours a pink jet of bubble bath under the hot rush.

"Wanna take a bath?"

I stroke a gold towel rack. "I really need to talk to you."

"We can talk in the tub." She traces my cheek with her finger. Goose bumps form down my arms.

"Well, um…okay."

I sit on the toilet seat cover while the tub fills. Lindsay sweeps assorted tubes of creams, makeup brushes, bottles of nail polish off the counter and into a drawer. She shoves crumpled lingerie and damp towels into a clothing hamper.

While Lindsay goes to get fresh towels, I quickly undress, easing my thin body into the intense heat. Bubbles pop and my cold toes burn. I lean back, my limbs melting.

Lindsay returns with fluffy beige towels. "How is it?"

"Heavenly."

She pulls her hair into a loose ponytail on top of her head and starts unbuttoning her pajama top. I gaze at her, my eyes riveted as she reveals one shoulder, then the other, swiveling her hips as she maneuvers the shirt down her back, revealing her breasts. I draw in my breath. She fluffs her hair and arches her back, one leg resting on the edge of the tub. I sink a little lower in the water as she slides her pajama bottoms over her hips. She kicks them aside and steps into the tub, settling her flushed skin across from me. She rubs her hand up the arch of my foot. "I told you I wanted to be a stripper."

I swallow. "Very professional."

"I could teach you." Her hand inches up my calf to my knee.

"I don't think it's my thing. I have other, less dangerous, career plans."

"I like danger." She kneads my quad, inching up my leg.

I swallow again, my muscles tightening. "Yes, I know you do."

Her fingers stop. "What's that supposed to mean?"

I swallow.

Lindsay raises one eyebrow.

I hesitate. "I saw you that other day, getting into that guy's car."

She pauses, her face relaxing. "So, what about it? You should come with me."

"No, thanks." I pull my leg away from her up to my chest.

"It'd be fun—"

"With some guy?"

"What's wrong with guys?"

"Nothing, nothing's wrong." I sit upright in the tub, my breasts popping out of the water. I cross my arms over my chest. "Why'd you want to go with, with strangers?"

"It's fun. I get to disappear for a while." Lindsay leans back in the tub.

"Disappear from what?"

"From this house, my school, my name even." She splashes water over her shoulders.

And from me, from our girl-hips rocking tight like waves?

I climb out of the tub, wrap myself in one of the towels. I sit on the edge of the tub and scratch my knee. Lindsay looks down at the bubbles.

"I wish you wouldn't do it."

"Why?"

"Because…" I look at Lindsay's scowling face. Because you're mine. "Because…it's dangerous," I blurt.

She laughs. "I know. It's not like I do anything with those guys. I just get lifts."

I stare at her. "I…I…don't want you to do that anymore."

Lindsay's eyes narrow. The air between us hangs thick and humid like a cloud of rain, heavy and gray. She slaps her hand against the water. "I don't want to talk about it." Her eyes flash storm clouds. She climbs out of the tub, heavy-breasted and flushed, rubs her body down with a fluffy towel. She leans over and presses her lips hard against mine, too hard, nips my lip. "Just don't," she says. "Just don't."

We get dressed silently and head back downstairs. My tights are wet on my thighs, my skirt clinging to my legs.

I slip on my boots at the front door. "I think I'll go now."

"I'll walk you to the subway."

"You don't have to do that."

"I don't mind." Lindsay's eyes are still and calm.

"It's still raining."

"I was planning on going out anyway."

I wait for her to lace up her boots.

When we turn down Yonge Street, she says, "Let's walk a little longer." I hesitate before following her toward Bloor. A few meters past the bus stop Lindsay undoes her coat, climbs onto a snowbank and sticks out her arm.

"What are you doing?"

"Wait."

I watch from the other side of the snowbank. An older man with a mustache waves. Lindsay backs away, leans against a lamppost.

"Forget it. I'm going."

"Just wait a minute."

Another car stops, a red sedan driven by a young guy. He rolls down the window. "Where are you going?"

Lindsay leans into the car. "Depends."

He has longish, greasy, blond hair and a sly smile. He blinks his blue eyes. "I'm heading uptown."

She looks back at me. "Perfect, right?"

I fold my arms across my chest. The guy unlocks the car door. "Aren't you coming?"

I back away. "Neh, I've got stuff to do."

"Oh, c'mon. I dare you."

I shiver in my wet tights, the rain still falling.

"I double-dog dare you." Lindsay smiles her teasing grin. She slides one hand down her hip, glancing over at the guy in the car, her shoulder coming up to rub against her cheek.

"No, I'm not playing."

Lindsay shrugs and starts climbing down the snowbank into the car.

"What are you trying to escape from anyway?" I ask.

Lindsay whirls around. Her face falls. She looks flustered. "Nothing." She gets in the car and gazes up at the guy. She is no longer teasing and confident, but looks younger, more vulnerable. I take a step back, recoiling.

The car swerves into traffic, spraying me with slush. I stare after it until it disappears in the maze of lights and traffic. Vehicles roar up the street; people brush by me on the sidewalk; a dog stops to sniff my damp legs.

I stand on the street, stunned. That look on Lindsay's face, I've never seen it before. She's trying to escape from herself.

I know it: She doesn't like herself. I've never seen her like that, unconfident, or weak. My mouth fills with a bitter taste. All along I've admired Lindsay, wanted to be like her, but not now. She doesn't have any idea what it really means to escape, what sacrifice it entails.

I wipe the slush off my coat with my mitten and start running up Yonge Street, my feet slipping on the melting snow. My arms pump as I weave through side streets.

When I get home I run up to my room. Neshama follows me. "Abba was wondering where you were. I told them you stopped to talk to a friend."

"Fine." I slam the door in her face.

"Hey!"

"Go away."

"They're waiting for you for lunch."

"Tell them I'm not hungry." I jam an old book under the door.

"Ellie?"

"GO AWAY!"

I rip down the poster of Joey McIntyre and start shredding it into tiny pieces.

"Ellie, someone saw you."

I yank open the door. "What do you mean?"

"I ran into Sari Blum on my way home. She saw you walking this morning. She asked me where you were going to *shul*. She said it looked like you were heading to the subway..."

I slump against the doorway. My stomach twists. "I don't feel well. Tell Abba I feel sick."

Neshama closes the door, and I crumple onto my bed. I'm taking crazy risks for a girl who would rather ride in cars with strange men. She's not worth it. No matter how much Lindsay makes me swoon, she isn't worth getting caught.

ON MONDAY I can't find my *Chumash*, and I forget my lunch at home. In the afternoon, I fail my Shakespeare test. On Tuesday I go straight home instead of to Lindsay's. When I get home there are two messages from her. I don't return them. I stare at my fish circling in their tank for a while, and then I reorganize my collection of fossils. Lindsay calls again on Wednesday, but I quietly hang up. On Thursday we get out of school early for Purim. I race home and erase two messages from Lindsay off the answering machine before anyone else hears them.

"What's with the phone calls?"

I lie on Neshama's bed watching her get dressed for Purim. "Nothing."

Her room is empty without the bears and music boxes. She even gave away the Harlequins from under the bed. Just her dresser is still messy—littered with makeup.

She pulls on a pair of black tuxedo pants, sings, "Don't cry for me Argentina."

"Why are you in such a good mood?"

"Just am. Do you want to be my lovely assistant?"

"Why, what are you?"

Neshama pulls on a tuxedo jacket and top hat. "Houdini." She holds out her arms. "I will now perform a magical disappearing act." She waves a tinfoil-covered chopstick and slips behind her closet door. "Ladies and Gentleman, Houdini has disappeared." She pops back out. "What are you going to be?"

"I'm not going."

She sits next to me on the bed. "They're starting to ask a lot of questions—about the phone calls, about where you go after school." She tries to read my face. I look out the window. "What's going on?"

"I can't tell you."

She squeezes my shoulder. "C'mon, Purim will be fun."

I groan. "Fine. Can you make me a costume?"

Neshama turns to her mirror and starts patting on face powder. "How about a cat?"

"Too boring."

"Bride?"

"For sure not."

"The Grim Reaper?"

"Too morbid."

"How about Queen Vashti?"

"No one wants to be her. She wouldn't even dance for the King."

"Yes, but she kept her self-respect," Neshama shoots back. She adjusts a black eye mask.

In the end I drape a white sheet over me and go as a ghost.

IN THE CHAPEL at Abba's school Neshama and I sit in the back row on the women's side, specially erected for Purim, listening to the chanting of the book of Esther.

Whenever the dreaded name of Haman is mentioned, the dressed-up, painted and inebriated crowd stomps and boos, rattling noisemakers, twirling small plastic *gregors*. A parade of tiny queen Esthers with shiny dresses and heavily made-up faces marches up and down at the front of the women's section. Miniature Mordecais with painted-on beards run in the aisle. I slouch in my folding chair, listlessly fiddling with my *gregor*.

Neshama clasps my hand. "I have something to tell you."

I turn to look at her, but I've lost my eyeholes. I lift my bum and twist the sheet.

"I got into university," she whispers.

The congregation stamps and yells. An adolescent boy stands on his chair, his face red from alcohol. He beats his chest, yodeling, "Yiyiyiyiyiiii" in a falsetto.

"That's great!" I hug Neshama and kiss her through the sheet, cotton against the hard plastic mask.

"Business?"

"Yes, but—"

"But what?"

Neshama pushes back the cuticle on her thumb. "I got into U of T and York, but I also got into the University of British Columbia and the University of Victoria."

"You applied away?" The congregation continues cheering, stomping Haman's name into oblivion.

"Uh-huh."

"Wow." I stare at her. "You're leaving?"

Neshama nods.

I hug her. "Wow, congratulations. Have you told Ima and Abba?" I glance at Ima a few rows up in her silk kimono and white face makeup. The congregation quiets down and the chanting continues.

She shakes her head. "Bubbie knows. She said she'd pay for it. The extra flights, living costs."

"That's amazing."

She nods again.

"Are you happy?"

"Yes. Sort of. Nervous and excited and I don't know..." She pauses. "Now I have to tell them." She gestures toward Ima with her head.

"What do you think they'll say?"

"That I'm going to burn in hell." Neshama's mask conceals her face. She clamps my hand in hers.

AFTER THE CHANTING, the chairs are pushed away and the dancing begins, the men in one circle, the women in another. At the back of the room, tables sag with baked goods and an immense bowl of alcoholic punch. Neshama and I nibble on poppy-seed *hamentaschen* and sip the tangy drink. The men form a tight circle, arms woven around shoulders, feet stamping in unison to a lively klezmer tune, clarinets blasting. A man dressed as a bride, a white veil covering his hair, his lips smeared with lipstick, is hoisted up and down on a chair.

"Oy, Oy, Oy, Oy!" he shouts. Backless high heels dangle from his thick feet. He blows drunken kisses as they put him down.

The women hold hands and whirl by, feet twisting and kicking. Dancers break off to form smaller inner circles. A woman dressed as a gypsy spins in the center, hips jiggling, her enormous bosom heaving. The women catcall and ululate in shrill voices. Tiny Queen Esthers worm their way through the swirling, stamping women and form their own small clapping circle around the gypsy lady. Ima spins by, laughing, taking tiny steps in her kimono.

"You really want to leave all this?"

Neshama finishes the rest of her punch, hiccups and shrugs. "Tradition is the illusion of permanence," she recites, her jaw firm.

"You won't miss it?"

"Nope."

I slump in my chair. "I really miss the Torah."

"So go back to it."

"I don't think I can."

"Maybe for you it doesn't have to be all or nothing. Make the Torah whatever you want it to be. It's so huge and contra-dictory, you can find whatever you want and ignore the other parts. Everybody does it."

"You think?"

"I know. Just don't take it as the word of God."

"Do you think Ima does?"

"Ima floats along in her own little world, taking in the parts that fit her life. Women can't sing in public—I bet she finds a way out of that one."

"And Abba?"

Neshama shudders. "He really does think the Torah is the word of God, but I try and cut him some slack because everything he does, misguided as it is, comes from his love for *Hashem*."

We both sigh. Then Neshama gets up and pulls me through the circle of dancing, stomping women, weaving into the center. Grabbing my hands she leans back and starts to turn. I shriek and pull back harder, the room spinning.

ON FRIDAY AFTERNOON when I leave school with Becca and Esther, Lindsay is waiting outside. My cheeks burn. Becca and Esther stare at Lindsay's short kilt and bare legs. "This is my friend from the summer," I mumble. "I'll catch up with you later."

"Bye, Ellie," they say. "Good *Shabbos*."

"What are you doing here?" I ask Lindsay when they walk away.

"I came to see you."

"You can't just come here." I guide her through the side alley to the bank parking lot.

"I waited for you to come over yesterday."

"It was a Jewish holiday. I had to go to *shul*."

"Well, you could've called."

"I didn't think you'd notice."

Lindsay looks at me skeptically. "You've come over twice a week for the past two months."

"Yeah, well, I'm sure you have better things to do, like ride in cars with boys," I mutter. I start walking down the side street.

"Do you have some time now? We could—"

"What?" I whirl around to face her. "Get in a car with some guys?"

"I just thought we'd talk—"

"I need to get home for dinner. We're having guests."

Lindsay follows me, walking quickly to keep up with my long strides. "I thought you stopped doing that."

I walk faster. "They decided to start again. You really need to get out of here."

She grabs my arm. "Look, about last time, I just thought it would be fun."

I stop. "Fun? What about me?"

"I like being with you too."

"That's it? Fun? I'm fun, like hitching, like boys?"

"Oh, c'mon, Ellie."

"Fun? Do you know what would happen if I got caught?" I stand on the corner, my mouth open, hands on my hips. "Do you have any idea how much I risk? You probably think it's funny. Ellie Gold: *yeshiva* girl by day, whore by night," I spit out the word. "You can do whatever dangerous stuff you like, but I can't."

"El—"

"You don't really even like me," I hiss.

Lindsay stares at me, mouth open. "I'll call you later."

"Don't bother. Ever."

I run across the street, leaving her standing on the corner.

Reaching home, I burst through the front door.

"You're late." Abba stands waiting in the front hall.

"Sorry."

"Where've you been?"

"Busy." I take off my coat and hat.

"Busy? Guests will be here soon."

"I was busy."

He glares at me. "What's the matter with you? You've been acting strange all week."

"Just leave me alone." I push past him to the hall closet.

"Hey!"

Ima peeks her head into the hall. "Ellie, just come and make the salad, okay?"

Abba follows me into the kitchen. Ima and Neshama are making meatballs, their hands sticky with raw hamburger. I sling my jacket and bag over a kitchen chair. Ima points to the tomatoes beside the cutting board. I pick up the knife.

Abba asks, "Neshama, did you vacuum?"

"You didn't ask me to."

"Can you do it now?"

"I need to finish getting ready."

His eyes flare at her. He turns to leave, and I hear the whirr of the vacuum cleaner a moment later.

"He's mad at me because I bought hors d'oeuvres instead of making them," Neshama says.

"What?" I stop chopping tomatoes.

"I said, Abba's mad at me because I didn't make the hors d'oeuvres. Are you okay? You look really pale."

"I'm fine."

Neshama digs her hands into a bowl of raw hamburger meat. "Ima, are you going to give a lesson tonight?"

Ima rolls the cold meat into a sphere and drops it in a pot of simmering tomato sauce.

"Your father's going to talk instead."

"What?" Neshama spins around.

My hand slips, the knife nicking my knuckle. Blood dribbles out of the cut.

"He has something to say."

"About dating?" Neshama asks.

"I'm not sure."

"Ima!"

I run my finger under cold water.

"What did you do?" Ima asks.

"It's nothing."

"Here." Neshama gives me a napkin.

"Let me finish that." Ima takes the knife from me. "Go shower." She looks at me carefully. "Are you sure you're okay?"

I mumble, "Yes."

In the bathroom, I turn the shower on and let the water beat down on my scalp. I wish it were a rainstorm in China, a monsoon, hot drops falling in sizzling heat. I put the stopper in the drain and let the water build around my feet. I wish it were a flood, water crashing over banks, ripping though fields, wrenching trees, my body snatched by a wave. Tears sneak down my face.

When I get out, Neshama thrusts the phone into my hands. "Call her."

"What are you talking about?"

She follows me into my room. I plug in my hairdryer and start fluffing my hair. "She called twice when you were in the shower." Neshama yells over the noise.

I freeze and click off the dryer.

"I answered both times, and then Abba unplugged the phone."

I relax.

"Ellie, she's going to call when *Shabbos* is over."

"I don't want to talk to her."

"She'll keep calling. They'll get suspicious."

Neshama pushes the phone into my hands and closes my door.

I sit down on the bed, wrapped in my towel, and dial Lindsay's number.

"Hello?"

"Hi, it's me."

"Finally."

"Look, you can't call here anymore."

"I was wondering when you'd—"

"You're not even in love with me, are you?" The word furls off my tongue before I can stop myself. I curl up in a ball on the bed.

Lindsay doesn't say anything.

"Then just forget it," I say. "Please stop calling."

"Can't we just be friends?"

I smirk. "You don't get it. I don't want just a friend. I want a...a..." I can't say the word. "It's not a game to me. It's not tag, or hide-and-go-seek, or dare. This is who I am." I want to say I deserve more, but this sounds like something you'd hear on a talk show about personal growth. "Aren't I more important than boys in cars? Aren't I?" I demand.

Lindsay doesn't answer. I want her to say, Yes, of course. I want her to tell me that she loves me. She won't. Lindsay doesn't love me. A sob rises up my throat. I wait another moment and hang up the phone.

Neshama knocks softly on the door. "Can I come in?"

"Go away." I sob silently, my chest heaving.

She pushes open the door and sits next to me, wrapping her arms around me. My tears stain the front of her yellow blouse. She strokes my wet hair.

"I thought you had a crush on Joey McIntrye."

I start to hiccup.

"What about Bo from *Days*? And Danny Durschwitz?"

I start to laugh, still crying. I wipe my chin with the back of my hand.

Neshama passes me a tissue. "The guests are going to be here any minute."

I nod and blow my nose.

THE GUESTS ARE similar to the ones from the fall: a few young men, but mostly women in modest clothing, eager to learn. Abba leads the blessings, Neshama and I bring out soup and salad and clear dishes. Ima serves meatballs. I eat without tasting my food, barely listening. I remove more dishes, help bring out dessert and tea. When Neshama and I start clearing the last dishes, Abba stops us.

"Wait," he says, "I want to show you something." He clears all the dishes onto the sideboard except one teacup, which he places in the center of the table. Neshama and I gape at Abba as he walks around the table, flapping each corner of the tablecloth, shifting the crumbs toward the cup. He scoops the crumbs into the cup with his fingers. "There," he says, and places the nuts and fruit back on the table, a pleased expression on his face. "All clean."

Neshama gives him a skeptical look.

"Come, sit down." He pats the chair next to him. Neshama and I sit automatically, the other guests resuming their seats.

"Neshama," my father begins.

"Yes?"

"Tell me, what are the things prohibited on the Sabbath?"

Neshama stares at him. Abba hasn't tested us like this in years. "All work, including sowing, reaping, gathering, winnowing, food preparation—"

"Ah, what is winnowing?"

"Winnowing?"

"Yes, what is it?" The guests gaze curiously at Abba and Neshama.

She pauses. "I have no idea. I've only been taught to memorize, not—"

"Let me explain." He leans forward, knuckles on the edges of the table. "Winnowing involves beating the wheat to release the kernels. Yes?"

Neshama nods.

"Tell me, Neshama, is this work?"

"Yes, Abba."

"And may we work on *Shabbos*."

"No, Abba." Neshama stares straight ahead, avoiding the guests' eyes.

"Very good. Now, tell me, when we shake out a tablecloth on *Shabbos* eve, are we not releasing the crumbs from the cloth as if we were winnowing?"

Neshama grimaces. "I suppose you would think so."

"Then should we consider shaking this tablecloth to be work?"

"I guess," Neshama says slowly. "In your opinion, but—"

"Then"—Abba slips into a sing-song, his right thumb coming up to accent his point—"by scooping up the crumbs like I showed you, we have found another way to keep God's word. And when we are closer to Him, then we are closer to bringing *Moshiach*." He smiles at the guests around the table. They tenuously smile back at him.

Neshama's mouth settles into a hard tight line until her lips disappear altogether. She perches on the edge of her chair.

When the guests have left and Neshama and I are alone in the kitchen, I whisper, "If we all just sang and didn't worry about crumbs, wouldn't *Moshiach* come faster?" Neshama glares at me and marches into the dining room where Abba is still sitting with his prayer book. She yanks off the tablecloth, sending salt and pepper shakers tumbling, knives clattering, dirty forks flying onto the carpet. She whips the tablecloth, ripping it through the air, the remaining crumbs scattering over the table and chairs. "Who cares," she yells, "who *fucking* cares?"

Ima pushes open the kitchen door.

Abba gawks, mouth open, eyes wide.

She flings the tablecloth on the floor at Abba's feet. "How dare you involve me in your crazy ideas? That's it. I'm finished with your religious crap. I'm leaving."

I crouch to gather the forks.

Abba stands up. "What are you talking about?"

Neshama gulps, clenches her hands. Her beautiful blond curls have come undone from her bun, descending down her back. "I got into Business at UBC and UVic."

Abba clutches his prayer book, his eyebrows shooting up. "BC? I thought you applied for programs here."

"I did, and away too."

Abba stands up. "How will you afford this?"

Neshama backs against the wall by the buffet. "Bubbie said she'd help."

Abba paces. "Where will you live?"

"In a dorm."

"With kosher food?"

"Oh, stop it. I'm *leaving*."

He stops pacing and looks at her for a long moment. Neshama glares back at him, arms crossed over her chest.

He turns and walks straight out the front door without his coat.

THE FOLLOWING WEEK I come home every day after school and catch up on all the homework I've missed. I keep myself busy so I won't think about Lindsay. When I do think about her, it's not lust or love I feel, but anger. I'm not imagining her skin or hair, but the look on her face in the car. I write a makeup test on Shakespeare. On Wednesday after school I drag Becca and Esther to an IMAX film on coral reefs, and in the evening I help Abba make muffins for a school bake sale. He doesn't talk to me the whole time, glowering in the flour. Neshama is almost never home. She even sleeps at Bubbie's one night.

FRIDAY AFTER SCHOOL, Ima asks me to go to *shul* with her.

"Which *shul*?" I ask.

"Just this one I've been going to for a while."

"What's it like?"

She pauses, thinking. "It's like, like one big burst of energy."

"Oh, well, sure…I guess so."

She smiles. "You'll like it."

Ima's *shul* is a nondescript building off Bathurst. We go up a narrow flight of stairs to a large multipurpose room, with a screen down the middle and rows of chairs. A modest ark sits on a wooden table at the front of the room. On the women's side a hallway leads to a bathroom and a small library where we leave our coats heaped on a table.

Ima and I choose seats in the middle.

"Why's it so quiet?"

"We're early."

A few women smile and nod to us as they take their seats. I notice the men's side has no chairs; the tops of the men's heads are visible over the thin screen. The room gradually fills up, grows crowded until there are not enough seats and young women stand at the back. Ima is the only woman wearing a scarf covering her hair. A few young mothers with babies wear stylish hats.

A voice from across the screen calls out, "*Mizmor Le David*," Sing the song of David; and voices rise around me, male and female, loud and vibrant, passionately chanting the first invocation of the start of *Shabbos*, the Psalm of David. Ima closes her eyes, her prayer book to her chest, her voice blending in with those around her. I haven't heard her sing since December.

"Sing the song of David, render his words unto him, and let peace into your soul." Her voice slides through me, breathy and passionate, making me shiver.

The week slips off me: Neshama and Abba's argument, their silence, Lindsay's phone calls and her silence. Voices harmonize around us. I start to hum, and the tension melts from my shoulders, my lips forming the words. I haven't prayed in months, not at school or at home.

The prayer ends, the tune melting into a psalm: *Yedid Nefesh*. I peer over the screen to see who is leading, but all I can see are rows of men's heads and a small red-headed child dancing wildly on the shoulders of a very tall man.

The room grows more crowded, heat pressing in. Girls in rows ahead take off sweaters and reveal thin bare arms, shoulders even.

We slip from prayer to prayer, one continuous burst of song-filled energy and passion. The tunes are new, but the words are the same. I close my eyes and let my voice resound with the others. I don't care what the words mean, I just want to sing.

When the singing stops I open my eyes and file out of the room into the cool spring evening. Sweat evaporates from my hair.

Ima kisses me. "*Shabbat Shalom.*" We stand on the pavement watching people greet each other. We start the long walk home.

"That was really different," I say. We head up the hill on Bathurst, cars whizzing by.

Ima smiles at me. "The singing is good, isn't it?"

I nod.

"You can really feel the presence of *Hashem* there."

I shuffle my feet on the pavement, look down. "Ima." I clasp my hands behind my back. "Do you really believe in, you know, believe in God?"

"Of course I do."

"Even after what happened at Beth El?"

She blushes a little. "That's just people acting foolish."

I raise my eyebrows.

She sighs. "Look, this is the way I think about it. God—it's a hard concept. Think of it as just a force."

"A force?"

"Yeah, like gravity. You believe in gravity, right?"

"Yeah, sure."

"Well, that's all God is."

I crinkle my brow. "Something that holds us on the earth? That doesn't make sense at all." I swing my hands down against my thighs. "You can measure gravity—you use Newtons or whatever—but you can't measure God."

Ima nods and doesn't speak. She stops at the intersection to wait for the traffic to clear. "Do you believe in love?"

"Pardon?"

"Do you believe in love?"

"Yeah, sure."

"Can you measure that?"

I swallow. "I guess not."

"How do you know you're feeling it?"

I think about Lindsay in her kilt and sweater running down the halls of her house. I miss her bitterly. I shake my head and concentrate on Ima. "You just do."

"So, what's the difference? We can't measure love, but we never deny its existence."

The traffic light changes, and Ima starts walking. I pause on the sidewalk. We can't measure love, but we never deny its existence. And God? I jog to catch up to her. "I don't get it. It's just the same?"

"Well, that's the way I think of it."

"And science?"

Ima looks at me. "Sure. Love, science—I don't think there's much difference. Do you want to walk through the ravine?"

The light is starting to fade around us. "We'll have to walk fast."

We head down the slope to the path. The snow has melted and the earth looks raw and tired, dark piles of mulch, rotted leaves tamped down.

"In Jerusalem," Ima continues, "when we walked to *shul* you could see the whole city quieting down, everyone getting ready for rest, the traffic thinning out. I loved that."

"Ima, what you said about God and love, you think it's in all love?"

"Sure. I think so, don't you?"

I kick some rotted leaves. "Even if you love the wrong person?"

"Oh, I don't think there's any such thing."

"Really?"

"As long as they don't hurt you."

"And if they do?"

She glances at me. I squirm. "Then you leave. Fast." I avoid looking at her. "I still think love is always good. I loved being in California, and I don't think it was the right thing for me, but I still felt loved there."

"Do you ever think about going back?"

Ima looks up at the trees, shrugs her shoulders. "I want to be somewhere quiet, somewhere without traffic and, you know, people who judge, the Mrs. Bachners of the world maybe. But not there. I like that *shul*, just song and prayer." Ima grabs my hand and gives it a squeeze. "I'm really glad you came with me tonight. I knew you'd like it."

"The singing was good."

"We'll have to take Neshama or Abba."

"I don't think Neshama wants to go to *shul* anymore."

Ima's voice is sad. "I know."

The light around us dims into shadows, the bushes looming around us. "We'd better run if we're going to make it before it's really dark. Abba and Neshama will be waiting, hungry."

Ima nods and we pick up our pace, jogging along the dark path toward the streetlights at the top of the hill.

Ten

The week before school finishes in June, I come home Friday afternoon to find Ima, Bubbie and Neshama in the living room. Bubbie's silver hair is cut shorter, and her low neckline reveals a small diamond pendant. Her long nails are the same hot pink as her blouse and her high-heeled sandals.

"Hey," I say, "what's going on?"

"We're talking about Neshama's bright future in the business world." Bubbie pats Neshama's knee and gives me her brightest smile.

I look over at Ima. She is slumped in the wingback chair, her chin almost resting on her chest. She looks defeated, as if someone has socked her in the stomach.

Bubbie sighs and crosses her legs, dangling a sandal off her bare foot. "Annabelle, you have to be realistic. The girls don't want to be teachers. And not all people in finance work such crazy schedules. You can still be *frum* and make money. And really, how do you expect the girls to support themselves, or families, anyway?"

Ima ignores the jab at her and Abba's jobs. "Is this what you really want to do?" she asks Neshama.

Neshama nods.

"Oh," Ima says. She cranes her neck around to look at me. "Ellie?"

"Fish," Neshama says, before I can respond.

"Pardon?" Ima asks.

"She wants to study something to do with fish and rocks," Bubbie explains.

"A zookeeper," Neshama offers.

"Oceanographer," Bubbie says.

"Ellie?" Ima asks.

I pause in the doorway. "Echinoderms," I murmur. I taste the shape of the word on my lips. I have never said it aloud before. I've never been asked what I want to do.

Bubbie continues, "Ellie should take night school courses, in addition to her regular school. Maybe in the fall."

I whisper, "Geology," like it's holy. I feel like I might swoon.

"The girls need to follow their interests," Bubbie says. "You know, explore. Just like you did. Turkey for you. University for them."

Ima blushes slightly. "I went to university."

"You didn't finish."

"Tell us about Turkey, Ima," Neshama says.

"Oh, you've heard it a million times."

"Well, then, how about the nun stage?" Bubbie suggests.

"Yes, the nun stage!" Neshama exclaims.

I sit down on the sofa next to Neshama. "Why did you want to be a nun?"

"I liked the idea of silence."

"That and being the bride of Christ." Bubbie crosses herself.

"It was a very spiritual place."

"So why didn't you stay?" I ask.

"I was going to—"

"But her father swore he'd never talk to her again," Bubbie says.

"He was always threatening that," Ima says.

"He wouldn't have been able to talk to you if you were in a silent convent," Neshama adds.

"That's true."

"So, what happened?"

"I met your Abba."

Neshama frowns. "That always happens just when a story is getting good. Some guy shows up and that's the end."

If it's not a guy, then how does the story end?

The front door opens and we hear Abba call, "Shalom."

"We're all in the living room," Bubbie replies.

Neshama darts into the kitchen and closes the swinging door. "I'm not here," she whisper-hisses.

"Good evening. What's going on?" Abba looks suspiciously at us.

"Ellie wants to study fish," Ima says to him.

"Rocks and volcanoes too," I add. I feel giddy with possibility.

"Rocks?"

"Uh-huh." I turn myself upside down, hair hanging on the floor, long legs dangling over the armrest. "Not only sedimentary and igneous, but volcanic." I think of hot lava pouring over a volcano's edges. "Did you know…?" I swing myself back upright. "You can tell the age of the earth? And it's old, so old it's even older than…it's absolutely ancient."

"We think Ellie should take night school courses next fall—you know, geology," Bubbie explains.

Abba drums his fingers on the doorjamb. "These rocks and fish, how will they make you live better?"

"Oh, Avram, it's not about that," Bubbie says.

"Ellie," he says, sitting down next to me, "if it's not about that, what good is it?"

Neshama sticks her head in the room. "It's not for her soul. It's for her mind. So it grows and expands."

"And you can't do that with Torah?"

"You can."

"So?"

"It's just not the only way."

"But it's the best way."

"For you maybe," Neshama says.

Abba doesn't say anything, and again I see them locked eye to eye.

"Neshama is only half right," I say softly. They turn to look at me. "Volcanoes and rocks, they're science, but *Hashem* created them, right? And if we don't learn to protect them, then we are ruining God's creations. That's got to be from the *Sitra Achra*, right?"

Abba smiles at me, laughs out loud. "A tongue she has," he says, rubbing his hands together. "With it you will argue Torah well," he announces.

"And what about fish and rocks?" Bubbie says.

"Maybe it's all the same," I say. "Maybe." My mind reels. They all stare at me. "A geologist could help heal the earth. What better job could there be?" I back out of the room. "Excuse me, I need to do something." I lope up the stairs to my room, grab the canister of fossils and my *Chumash* out of my backpack and start rifling through the pages. Yes, a geologist heals the earth. This is Torah.

I spend the afternoon in the backyard underneath the chestnut tree with my back pressed up against its trunk, reading through Deuteronomy for specific passages. I mark them with my pencil and fold the corners of the pages. From the house I hear Ima and Abba getting ready for *Shabbos*. Bubbie has invited herself for dinner and is making salads in the kitchen. I ignore Abba's requests for help, pretending not to hear him. Gently I spill the canister of fossils across the open pages of my *Chumash*. I finger them, imagine the heat they've been exposed to, the pounding water carving that enormous depth in the middle of desert, sand stretching across the horizon, layered like a cake. I squeeze the shells tight. I've got love in my fingers, ocean in my hands, gravity here in my palms.

And protecting the land, all the lands, this has to be Torah.

WE ARE A silent, cautious group around the *Shabbos* table. I can hear birds singing from the yard through the open windows as we do the blessings. Neshama wears a short-sleeved T-shirt with her long skirt. Abba stares at her bare arms.

"So," Bubbie says, "I was thinking I'd help Neshama get settled out in Vancouver."

"That would be fine." Abba's voice is formal. "Thank you."

"And I was thinking Ellie could come along, make a holiday of it."

I sit bolt upright. "I get to go? To the sea?"

"If your parents allow you to go—"

"Oh, please, please, please." I leap out of the chair and kneel by Abba. "Please let me go. I'll wear whatever you want, and I'll only eat kosher and—please."

Abba stares at me, eyes uncertain. "I'll think about it."

"Abba, I *have* to go."

"Why are you so anxious?"

"It's the sea."

"She's been dying to go forever," Neshama says.

"You know, the fish thing," Bubbie explains.

"She has asked to go for years," Ima adds.

"Enough, *sha*. I said I'd think about it."

"It's fine with me, Ellie."

I turn to Ima. "Really?"

"Sure. You went away with Bubbie last summer and it was fine, wasn't it?"

I blush.

"Yes, it was excellent," Bubbie says. "We had a great time, didn't we? We'll get your sister settled in Vancouver, and after that we'll head to Vancouver Island and explore the seashore for creatures."

I do a small dance, wiggling my hips and shoulders. "I'm going to the sea!"

I'll see rocks eroded by waves in small whirlpool clefts.
I'll peer into tide pools and see hermit crabs scuttle, the stillness followed by the sudden dart of tide pool sculpin. Bull kelp
will wave in long tangly strands, and the shore will be squishy
with rock lettuce. And when the tide goes really far out I'll be
able to find sea stars and sea cucumbers and...and...and...
"Check it out." I pull up my sleeve and flex for Neshama,
grunting. Abba's mouth falls open. Ima breaks into laughter.

"So, I can go, Abba, please?"

He looks down, moves his fork across his plate.

"What are you so worried about?" Bubbie folds her arms
across her chest.

"I kept kosher last time. And I prayed and kept *Shabbos*."

"I'm worried about other things."

"Well, what?"

Abba blushes.

Ima glances at him. "You're worried about boys. That's it,
isn't it?"

Neshama spits a mouthful of red wine onto her dinner plate.

"I'm an excellent chaperone," Bubbie says. "We had no
problems last summer."

Neshama starts to giggle so hard she chokes. I grab her
arm and, pounding her back, drag her into the kitchen.

"I'm sorry, Ellie," she snorts.

"Shhhh!"

I stand behind the closed, swinging door.

"Let's do the final scene from *Dirty Dancing*," she says. "You
be Baby—go sit in the corner—and I'll be Patrick Swayze."

"I'm trying to listen."

"Don't worry, you'll get to go. As long as you promise, no boys." She slaps a hand against her thigh.

"Shut up." I elbow her in the ribs. She gets me in a head-lock, rubs her knuckles over my scalp. I pull away, trying to tickle her. She whoops, giggling. We knock over a chair.

"Girls?" Bubbie swings the door open.

We look up, still wrapped around each other, tittering. Our hair is mussed, our clothes askew.

"What are you doing?"

"Wrestling." I pin Neshama against the wall by the phone.

Bubbie pauses. "Oh, well, I have to go. Canasta," she says loudly. Then she whispers, "Before they start praying again." She points toward the dining room.

Neshama wriggles one arm out of my grasp. "You won't stay for dessert?"

"No, stop by tomorrow. We'll talk about our trip."

I let go of Neshama. "I get to go?"

Bubbie nods.

I fling my arms around Bubbie, smack a noisy kiss on her rouged cheek. Neshama stumbles and squeezes her arms around the both of us.

"Okay, enough with the love." Bubbie grimaces.

"Love, a force like gravity!"

"What?"

"Never mind. Wanna see my triceps?" I roll up my sleeve. Bubbie pokes my arm. "Wow. Push-ups?"

"Yep."

We kiss Bubbie good-bye and bring the fruit platter into the dining room.

Ima looks at me. "You can go."

"Thank you." I wrap my arms around her and give Abba a quick kiss on the cheek.

"You're welcome." She dishes pineapple out onto plates.

"What are you guys going to do this summer?"

"I'm teaching a summer course," Abba says. He looks at Ima. "Nu?"

Ima doesn't answer.

"Are you going to tell them?" he asks.

Ima blushes and puts down her fork. "I have a new plan."

I freeze, fork in midair. "For what?"

"You know, helping people be more observant."

"What's that?" I ask.

"I'm going to be teaching a class about women and Judaism this fall."

I look at Abba. He smiles at us.

"More anti-dating?" Neshama asks.

"Yes, and other things too." Ima hesitates. "I'd like one thing from all of you before the summer. I want you to come to *shul* with me. My *shul*."

"That's it?" Neshama blurts out.

"That's it."

Neshama nods. "No problem."

"Avram?"

"What kind of *shul*?"

"Orthodox."

He pauses. "I'll think about it."

AFTER DINNER, NESHAMA and I head to the back porch. The chestnut tree is in bloom, the leaves green and full, the blossoms small white tufts like popcorn. Next door the forsythia in Mrs. Fidderman's yard has already bloomed. Magnolia petals litter her lawn.

We sit on the stairs, drinking tea. A warm breeze blows, ruffling our hair.

"Ellie, why do you want to be near the sea? You've never even seen it."

"It's not just the sea. I want to see tide pools."

"Shells and seaweed?"

"Yes, but also jellyfish and sea stars, red and purple and—"

"But what do you like about it?"

"Well…" I draw my knees into my chest. "The sea is never the same. Each time the tide comes in, it's different. And when the tide changes, the plants and animals adjust." Neshama raises her eyebrows. "Like seaweed. It retains water and stays damp."

"That interests you? Dampness?"

I sigh. "No, I like the way it…fluctuates."

"So you're just interested in the change?" Neshama looks at me skeptically.

"Well, yeah, and that it finds a new equilibrium. Balance."

"It changes and it's the same?"

"Exactly."

Neshama groans.

"Look at this." I pull out the canister of shells Ima brought from Israel and pour them into my hand.

"What about them?"

"Ima found them in the middle of the desert."

"Yeah, so?"

"Well, that means the ocean was there once."

"And?"

"Well, it's like the stamp of *Hashem*."

"Oh, don't start with the God crap."

"No, this is huge. Forget the Bible and Abba's rules. There are shells in the desert. Don't you get it? The ocean and land came before all that."

"Didn't you already know that, dinosaur girl?"

"Yes, but it doesn't matter who owns it or puts up buildings. *Hashem* is first in nature, not in the temples or laws done in his honor."

"And that's why you want to see the ocean?"

"Partly, and 'cause it's beautiful."

Neshama flicks her hair over her shoulder. "If you say so."

We're silent a moment. "I think I'll climb the tree." I put my mug down on the porch.

Neshama watches me swing myself up into the arch of branches, settle in the crook of the tree.

"You know what I want?" I say.

"What's that?"

"I want everything Ima says about how to get married."

"You do?"

"Yep."

"El, you don't want to marry some *yeshiva bucher* Abba chooses for you."

"That's not what I mean. I want someone to say, 'I think I know someone who'd be perfect for you.' I'd like to meet that person and talk to them until I know if they are my *b'shert*."

"And if they are?"

"Then I'd hold their hand."

"You're a nut."

"No, I'm not." I pull a chestnut leaf off the tree, carefully tear it along its threads.

Neshama tips her head. "What Ima said is about men."

"Not necessarily."

"Ellie, gimme a break."

"So it's a little unconventional. You never know."

"You're practical and yet *such* a dreamer." Neshama stands up.

"I want everything."

"And you think you can have it?"

"I think I can."

Neshama smiles and shakes her head.

I want a nice girl in a long purple dress, who likes trees and who knows all the *Shabbos* blessings. I want a girl with hair and legs like Lindsay, someone as smart as Neshama and with as wicked a tongue as Bubbie. And we'll live by the sea.

THE LAST DAY of school dawns sticky and hot. "I'm never wearing this uniform again!" Neshama twirls across the kitchen, her skirt fanning out. She rolls it over at the waist until her knees show.

"I have a surprise for you," I say.

"Uh-huh." Neshama digs into a grapefruit.

"Just you wait."

"Sure." Neshama bounces in her chair.

"I have a question you're going to like for Q and A."

"Really?" She puts down her spoon. "You're not going to ask—"

"Maybe."

"Tell me."

I smile and turn away.

"Ellie." She stands up and grabs my waist, starts tickling me.

"Okay, okay, stop. It's about the land, the land."

"You mean why it's only for us?"

"No."

"What then?"

"You'll have to wait." I stick out my tongue.

We file into the *beit hamidrash* after lunch, our voices louder than usual. Since we don't have classes during the summer, Rabbi Lowenstein always tries to talk about *T'sha B'Av*, the day of mourning for the fall of the Temple on the last day of the school. No one can muster the proper mourning attitude because of the holidays.

"Are there any questions?" Rabbi Lowenstein scans the rows of girls. The back of my skirt sticks to my thighs, the vinyl seat hot and sweaty. The fans above swirl the humid air. Traffic noise wafts through the open windows. Rabbi Lowenstein's eyes rest briefly on Neshama. I hesitate before raising my hand. All eyes turn to me. "Ellisheva, a question? Good." He smiles and beckons for me to come up to the podium.

I take out my *Chumash* and get my notes out of my skirt. I rest my shaking hands on the flat wooden surface. Neshama watches me, her hands tucked under her knees, her blue eyes intent. I smile at her, take a deep breath and spread my notes in front of me.

"I want to ask about what the Torah has to say," I pause, clearing my throat, "about the land, about how we are polluting our air, water and land. I've been trying to find some answers in my *Chumash*. At first glance, I don't think the Torah is very concerned with how we treat the land at all, just that as Jews we claim it as a people as our own. I know people weren't worried about the environment back then, they were nomadic, but I did come up with some helpful passages."

I glance at Reb Lowenstein. He nods for me to continue.

"For example, if you'll turn to *Shofetim* 20:2, you'll see it outlines rules for protecting trees during times of warfare."

I look up at Neshama. She beams back at me.

IN THE EVENING, the fading sun slants across the folding chairs at Ima's synagogue. A warm breeze blows through open windows. We stand for the prayers, Ima on my left and Neshama on my right. Ima sings, "*Havou le donai.*" Praise the Lord, and Neshama's voice rises with hers. I turn to stare at her, listening to her voice low and sweet, climbing around the notes. I join in too. Ima's smile stretches wide, her eyes sparkling. Neshama winks at me, and turns to show me her fingers tightly crossed behind her back. Abba's head looms just over the screen, bearded and flushed with the heat.

I hear his voice loud and gruff with ours, *"Mizmor le David,"* Sing the song of David.

Rows ahead I notice a girl, her brown shoulders exposed in a tank top. Springy black curls tumble down a lithe neck and brush against muscular arms. She turns around, catching my eye. She has sparkly brown eyes, dark skin and full cheeks. Heat climbs up my face, my arm hairs rising. I don't look away.

Glossary

Abba—father

Amidah—set of eighteen prayers recited daily by observant Jews

Ba'al T'shuva—literally "one who has returned." A formerly non-observant Jew who returns to the traditional ways of Judaism (also means reborn Jews).

Barchu—a Jewish prayer

Baruch Hashem—"Praised be God"

B'shert—a person destined to be your soul mate

Beit HaMidrash—a study hall

Benchers—a small book containing the Prayer After Meals and other songs sang on the Sabbath or other joyous occasions

Bochel—a fat tummy

Brucha—blessing

Chachkas—knickknacks

Challah (challot)—braided bread(s) eaten on the Sabbath

Cholent—a bean and meat stew traditionally eaten on the Sabbath. It is prepared before the Sabbath to avoid having to cook on the day of rest.

Chumash—the five books of the Pentateuch, often referred to as the five books of Moses. The word "chumash" is from the Hebrew word meaning "five."

Chuppah—a wedding canopy under which a marriage ceremony is conducted

Chutzpadik—nerve or gall

Daf Yomi—a daily regiment to study a page of Talmud. With this regimen the entire Talmud would be studied in seven and a half years.

Daven—to pray

Drash—an interpretation of a biblical text

D'var Torah—a talk on topics relating to a section of the Torah

Eishet Chayil—literally "A woman of valor." This poem is frequently sung to a wife by her husband on the Friday night of the Sabbath.

Frum—religious or observant

Goyische—a derogatory word for a non-Jew

Gregors—noisemakers used on the Jewish festival of Purim

Halacha—Jewish law

Hamentaschen—a three-cornered cookie filled with prunes or poppy seeds that is traditionally eaten on the holiday of Purim

Hanukah—the annual Jewish festival, also known as the Festival of Lights, celebrated over eight successive days. Hanukah commemorates the rededication of the Temple of Jerusalem by Judas Maccabee in 165 BC.

Has va'halila—"Heaven Forbid," an expression of horror

Hashem—God

Havdalah—a ceremony marking the end of Sabbath using candles, wine and sweet spices

Ima—mother

Kallah v'chatan—bride and groom

Kippah—religious head covering worn traditionally only by men

Knishes—a pastry stuffed with potato or other savory filling

Kol Isha—literally "the voice of a woman." This refers to the Jewish law that forbids a woman from leading prayers for men, or for a woman performing for men.

Kosher—Jewish dietary laws

Kotel—part of the massive remaining stone walls of the Second Temple. The Kotel is also called the Wailing or Western Wall and is the most sacred site in Judaism.

Kugel—a noodle casserole

Latkas—potato pancakes, traditionally eaten at Hanukah

Mazel Tov—"Congratulations"

Mezuzah—a parchment inscribed with a religious text and attached in a case to the door posts of Jewish homes as a sign of faith

Mincha—the afternoon prayers

Mishnah—the oral tradition of Jewish law. The Mishnah was the first important work of rabbinic Judaism.

Minyan—ten men (or in some synagogues, ten men or women) needed for public worship

Mikvah—a ritual bath used for purification

Mishigas—nonsense

LEANNE LIEBERMAN

Moschiach—the Messiah

Parsha—a portion of the Hebrew bible

Pogrom—an organized massacre directed against a particular group

Purim—a joyous Jewish holiday that commemorates the deliverance of Persian Jews from the plot of the evil Haman to exterminate them. This story is recorded in the biblical Book of Esther.

Rosh Hashanah—the Jewish New Year

Rugelach—a sweet pastry filled with chocolate, nuts or jam

Shabbat/Sabbath—the day of rest and worship. For Jews this is Saturday.

Shabbat Shalom—a greeting meaning happy or peaceful Sabbath

Shalom Aleichem—a song or greeting meaning "Peace Be Upon You"

Shiksa—derogatory term for a non-Jewish woman

Shivah—a period of seven days of mourning after the death of close relative. A family is said to be "sitting shivah."

Shma—the most important prayer in Judaism. It contains a passage from Deuteronomy and proclaims there is only one God.

Shonda—a disgrace or shame

Shul—a Yiddish word for synagogue or temple

Shulchan Aruch—literally "The Set Table." This is a book of Jewish law composed by Rabbi Yosef Karo in the sixteenth century.

Shvitz—to sweat

Siddur—a prayer book

Sitra Achra—literally the "other side"—refers to the forces of evil which underlie all of reality

Talmud—a record of rabbinic discussions pertaining to Jewish law, ethics, customs and history

T'sha B'Av—the ninth day of the Hebrew month of Av. This is a day of mourning for the fall of the temple and other atrocities in Jewish history. It is traditional to fast on this day.

T'fillah Ha'Derech—the prayer for safe travel

Toevah—an abomination

Torah—the law of God as revealed to Moses and recorded in the first five books of the Hebrew Scriptures. This is the first part of the Hebrew Bible.

Trafe—unkosher food

Tsur Mishelo—a song sung on the Sabbath thanking God for the food eaten on the Sabbath

Vayeshev—the ninth weekly Torah portion in the annual Jewish cycle of Torah reading

Yedid Nefesh—a psalm sung to welcome the Sabbath. It means "Beloved of the Soul."

Yeshiva Bucher—a yeshiva or seminary student

Yom Kippur—the Day of Atonement. Jews fast and ask for forgiveness from God and other people.

Yontif—means good day or holiday

Zai Gazunt—literally "Go in health"—the Yiddish way of saying "be well."

Zemirot—songs sung on the Sabbath

Leanne Lieberman grew up in Vancouver, British Columbia. Her work has previously been published in *The Windsor Review, The New Quarterly, The Antigonish Review* and other magazines. *Gravity* was Leanne's master's thesis at the University of Windsor. Leanne works as a teacher in Kingston, Ontario, where she lives with her husband and two sons.